Vampire Valley

Mountain City Chronicles Book 2

Alexander Nader

Hair Brained Press

Copyright © 2021 Alexander Nader All rights reserved

The characters and events portrayed in this book are fictitious. Any similarity to real persons, living or dead, is coincidental and not intended by the author.

No part of this book may be reproduced, or stored in a retrieval system, or transmitted in any form or by any means, electronic, mechanical, photocopying, recording, or otherwise, without express written permission of the publisher.

Cover design by: Pamela Nader

Printed in the United States of America

I love nothing more than hanging out with you, my reader. If any part of this story meant anything to you, or you just want to say it kicked ass or even if you hated it and feel the need to tell my big, dumb face, you can find me in any of these places. I'll always do my best to answer any questions.

Twitter: @AlexNaderWrites

Facebook: Facebook.com/alexnaderwrites

Instagram: @AlexNaderWrites

Website: https://alexnaderwrites.wixsite.com/my-site

Email: AlexNaderWrites@gmail.com

As a special thank you, anyone who signs up for the newsletter on my [website](#) will get a free ebook of Beasts of Burdin (The landing page says Necrotown, but since I'm guessing you've already read that, I'll make sure you get book 1 of my other series for being so awesome). I promise to never email you more than once monthly and will do my best to only include cool shit.

For my wife and kids, nothing fancy here, I love you all.

Alexander Nader

Chapter 1

Fox and I tear down the dirt road away from my birth, and rebirth, place. I turn on the high beams as the sun sets behind the trees. The power from my Faustian bargain crackles across my body. I intertwined my soul with a necromancer set on taking over the city. That's a good idea, right? Yeah, a brilliant fucking idea. There's a beautiful woman holding my hand and for the first time in a long time I feel alive.

If Sarah Roswell wants to take over Mountain City, she can damn well have the thing. Mountain city has been nothing but shit to me. I don't owe it a thing. Besides, Sarah's standard billionaire of a husband has been running the city into the ground for two decades now.

She better kill that bastard.

A flash of the mad mage's memory flashes before my eyes. My parents strung upside down, carved in mysterious runes and symbols. All so some rich dick could save his dying wife.

What would I do to save Fox if she were dying?

Fuck you, conscience. No one asked you here.

Fox squeezes my hand. I glance over at her, pale skin glowing blue in the light from the screen on the SUV's dash. Sune, the living fox tattoo that carries my wife's soul from body to body, jumps in circles around Fox's neck.

"You okay?" she asks.

"Yeah, I'm fine. Just…" What? Thinking about my dead parents?

She leans across the car and kisses my cheek. "You're thinking about something other than the sexy lady riding with you on the way to the beach with a bag full of cash."

"You know, that's a great point."

My wife, always the brains of the operation. I'm just the…all powerful, quasi-immortal arm candy? Am I all powerful now? Combining my soul with Sarah's gave us both an incredible well of energy to draw from, but I've only had that power for about twenty minutes, long enough to rip a mage in half with my bare hands. Not quite enough time to figure out the actual capabilities of this life and death magic shit.

Forget all that noise.

Fox is right. We have a bag full of Sarah's money and nothing but road in front of us. I focus on the road for the first time in miles. This is the road from my home, and I've driven it a million times. My body kind of knows the way. Blinking back into focus, we are ten minutes or so outside of downtown Mountain City. From there we can hit the interstate and be on the beach by sunrise.

I click on the radio. The first bars of Renegade by Styxx crackle through the speakers. I crank the volume and roll down my window. The air smells of honeysuckle, signs of summer. It's a damn fine time to leave, summer in Mountain City is hot as hell. We need to get somewhere with more water and less clothing.

"You good?" Fox's gaze bores into the side of my face.

"Yeah. Why wouldn't I be?"

"You got killed like four times and made a deal with a necromancer who exists from your parents' essence. I think you might be an all-powerful mage right now, and you sort of ripped a guy in half. It's kind of a spectrum of emotion you've run through in the past hour."

"Hey," I say. "I only got killed three times. The fourth was on purpose."

Fox huffs. "Either way. It's a lot."

"It is. Are you going anywhere?"

"Are you asking if I'm going to leave you?" Fox punches me. "No. Never, idiot."

"Then I'm just dandy."

"Good because it's no fun being at the beach with a pouty husband."

"Good point."

As we exit the mountains on the north side of the city, the dash chimes. The gas light flashes on the dash. The luxury SUV I stole from Sarah probably gets as much gas mileage as a fully loaded jumbo jet. Gas stations are going to be my new best friend.

There's a small corner market ahead on the right. The open light glows orange in the night.

I turn on the blinker. "We gotta put some gas in Charlaine."

"Charlaine, huh?" Fox smacks the dash. "I like it. And gas is good. We need cigarettes and snacks. Lots of snacks."

Always planning, she is. I park next to a pump. The lot is empty, other than a small Honda tucked away by the dumpster. Probably the employee's car. I reach into the back seat and grab a leather bag full of cash.

"How much do you think you need for gas and snacks?" I start counting out a couple twenties.

Fox snatches the thousand-dollar band of cash out of my hand. "This should do it. I'll let you know if I need more."

"Christ, woman. How many snacks are you buying?"

"I'm thinking one of everything with cheese in the name."

This woman. I lean across the car and kiss her. "Go wild, but get me a soda, too, please."

Fox hops into the parking lot. She does a little happy dance as she backs toward the entrance. Her sneakers are still covered in blood, my blood. If this new power is going to do anything, it better help me quit dying in front of my wife. That's real embarrassing.

"A huge one, from the fountain, with cherry," I shout across the lot.

The words are drowned out from bells as she pushes inside the store.

I grab the handle for the pump and start filling up with the cheapest swill the pump offers. This ain't my car and there isn't much chance of me driving it for another hundred thousand miles. Who cares what kind of gas it gets?

I cross my arms and lean against the side of the car. This is going to take forever. Wonder what's going to go faster, filling up the hundred-gallon tank or Fox picking out enough snacks to feed an army of toddlers. Probably the gas.

A cigarette would be great right now. Normally, I'd say a drink, too, but honestly, I feel the most level I have in a long time. The cigarette isn't even necessary, I just want the taste of the thing. Weird. Do high mages not get addicted? That can't be true, those fuckers drink like fish.

The gas station door chimes. I turn to see Fox walking out, two brown shopping bags overflowing with snacks bundled up like babies and giant drinks in each hand.

The pump clicks full.

The lady wins it by a hair.

As I put the handle back on the pump, a red light flashes across the sky.

"The fuck?"

A solid beam of light cuts through the dark, ending in an image of a wolf howling. Oh, shit.

"Is that…" I start.

Behind me, groceries fall to the pavement.

Ethan, the alpha of the Hairs and Fox's ex, gave Fox a warning beacon. He told her if she was ever in trouble and she shined it into the sky, the pack would come help. There were only two made, one for my wife and the other for Ethan, the pack looking out for its alpha.

The beam is close, maybe a mile east. It's hard to tell, but it looks south of Hair Nation, closer to downtown.

Fox rips her door open. "Get in. We gotta go help him."

There's no point in arguing. Fox has her mind made up. She still cares for Ethan and his people. All I want to do is go to the beach, but she'd never forgive me if we didn't help.

Ethan is the alpha and one tough son of a bitch. He wouldn't shine that light for fun. Something bad is going down and the big bad wolf needs help. I swear if this shit gets me killed and I have to drive back down this mountain all over again, I'm going to be so pissed.

Vampire Valley

I throw the SUV into gear and peel out of the parking lot, on my way to rescue my wife's ex who hates me. This isn't exactly the vacation I had in mind.

Chapter 2

My foot is to the floor. The SUV was built more for creature comfort than hauling ass, but Cadillac was still nice enough to shove a giant engine under the hood. The engine pushes to the redline, audible even in the heavy insulated interior.

Anxiety rolls off Fox in waves. I can practically taste her fear.

"Everything's going to be okay," I say.

"Uh-huh." Fox reaches into the back seat.

I put a hand on Fox's side to hold her in place as I take a sharp left toward the wolf signal. We aren't far now. The wolves will be coming from Hair Nation to help their alpha as well, but we were only a couple minutes away. The Hair compound is further north of the city. Depending on how fast their rides are, they are at least fifteen minutes away.

"Here." Fox sets a large handgun in my lap.

The thing looks like it's out of a Dirty Harry caricature, a gift from Ethan when we went mage hunting...Yesterday? Fuck, was that really yesterday? I need sleep. The gun only has 5 bullets left, after I used one to blow Bartholomew's leg clean off after he told me he oversaw the ceremony that killed my parents.

The gun is etched in runes. It seemed cool when I first touched it, but now, with a ten thousand volt hit of magic running through my veins, I can literally feel the weapon thrumming with energy. This thing could take out a high mage rhinoceros without a blink. The weapon calls to me, like a living thing calling my name. Stop, gun. I don't like that.

"Got anything smaller?" The gun doesn't have any extra ammo and I don't want to waste any bullets.

Fox slides back into her seat. She's got her orange katana gripped in her right hand, and my old snub nose revolver in the other. "That'll work fine."

"We don't even know what we're up against. It could be a false alarm."

Fox shoots a glare in my direction before turning back to watch the beacon. She doesn't even have to say anything. I know what the look was for. An alpha would never call a false alarm, would never intentionally look weak.

"There." Fox points.

The beam shines off to my right. It's coming from an abandoned strip mall parking lot. Back in the eighties, Charlie's Bucks and Burgers had the best venison burger I've ever tasted in my life. I used to go there for lunch at least three times a week. Charlie's was the life blood of the mall. Other businesses could ride off the customers coming in for lunch.

Charlie died of a heart attack in the late eighties. Some corporate place took over and the food went to shit. It didn't take long to figure out Charlie took his secret recipe with him to the grave. No Charlie meant no customers. An auto parts store almost made it to the new millennium, but fell short. The place has been empty ever since. Close enough to still technically be downtown, but far enough north that no one has any reason to be there unless they are heading into Hair or Sharp territory.

The tires screech as I whip into the parking lot. The ass end breaks loose from the sudden maneuver, but the SUV is so heavy it's a slow motion spin-out. I steer into the slide and make a full revolution before continuing toward the source of the light.

Three vans are parked in front of what used to be an office supply store. Figures move through the darkness, but I can't get a good look at anyone. They seem to be hovering around the source of the beacon.

I speed toward the group, loud enough for the engine to be heard. Fifty feet away, I slam the brakes and jerk the wheel hard right. The tires scream like they are running from an ax murderer. The car leans left and slides to a stop just outside the circle of people.

I unbuckle and jump out. Fox is around front before my feet hit the pavement.

The two figures closest to us turn and hiss.

Of course they fucking hiss.

Sharps.

Vampires.

Whatever you want to call them, they are weird as hell.

The two closest to us are wearing denim shorts and nothing else, no shoes, nothing. Their pale skin is covered in burned-on runes, protections from magic. Sharps hate magic. They refuse to have anything to do with the shit. Nothing magic is allowed in Vampire Valley. They are paranoid about it, so they cover themselves in anti-magic markings.

"Well, hello," the sharp to my right says to Fox. He licks his fang, showing off a pierced tongue in the process. "What do I gotta do to get a pretty little thing like you to invite me inside?"

Fox pulls her blade, but before the weapon is free I draw on the magic in the air. There's not much up here to use. It's too quiet, but the sharps definitely aren't touching the energy, so I've got it all to myself. I still have no idea the limits of my powers, but I guess it's time to start learning.

Mages are born with a natural inclination for magic. Even the greatest users spend most of their lives buried in books trying to master their craft. Anyone, even a Standard, can learn magic, but those born without the gift could spend a lifetime trying to master a single parlor trick.

I've studied magic some. As a quasi-immortal, I've been around more than a couple lifetimes and it gave me plenty of study time. Still, I could barely pull enough magic out of the air to light a cigarette before meeting Sarah Roswell. Now, it's like I've got a mainline into the central power grid.

In my head, I picture the asphalt under Tongue Ring's feet. Sharps have runes on their body to prevent magic from being directed at them, but I don't have to hit him with a lightning bolt to hurt the guy. I have no idea if my new magic requires hand motions, but to be sure I reach up and pull down like I'm trying to close a garage door. The ground beneath Tongue Ring opens up.

"What the—" he manages before falling through a hole in the ground.

I release my concentration and the asphalt returns to its normal state. Talk shit to my wife, get swallowed by a parking lot, fucker.

With the sharp out of the way, I can see the red beam coming from a keychain, gripped in the hand of a person laying flat on their back. More sharps are crouched down, cutting at him with ancient looking blades. Damn sharps and their carvings.

Fox isn't about to ask questions. With Tongue Ring gone, she doesn't hesitate as she closes the gap and slices off the head of Tongue Ring's denim-clad buddy. The sharp was too busy staring at the hole I created in the parking lot to even see her coming.

There's four more sharps standing. Another five are divided up between holding a half-dead alpha to the ground and carving shit across his chest and abdomen with curved blades.

A sharp with dreadlocks, bone white runes burned into his dark skin, looks up from carving something near Ethan's collar bone. He hisses some words. They either aren't in English or I don't catch them. Either from fangs or effect, sharps always seem to be hard to hear.

The four standing fangs split up. A dude in a leather jacket and a woman with a pink mohawk with burn scars down her arms thick as power cords move towards me. The other two flank Fox. One looks like a teenage girl, but markings cover her from forehead to ankles. So many markings, she's been around a lot longer than her pigtails suggest. The other is a guy, looks to be in his twenties. He's shirtless, and I only catch one rune etched into his chest. They sent the girl and the rookie after Fox, stupid bastards.

I turn my back on the teenie bopper and shirtless guy, Fox can handle them no problem. Leather Jacket and Mohawk move toward my sides. Classic vampire fighting technique, flank me. Eventually, I have to take my eye off one and the other will pounce like a rabid jackass. The giant gun is tucked into my waistband. The cold steel presses against my spine, the magic almost begging to be let loose.

Not yet.

Only five bullets left in the thing, there's no telling what things are worse in the night that a couple sharps.

I step back, keeping both enemies in sight. You make the first move, bitches.

They keep circling. As they get to the edges of my periphery, the wolf on the ground howls in pain. The sound is a guttural cry of agony that thrums in my chest. Instinctively, I turn to see what's happening.

Fucking mistake.

Both vampires lunge in tandem.

I duck under Mohawk. She sails past me and rolls across the pavement, landing in a crouch. Leather Jacket, however, went low. His shoulder catches me on the side of my hip, driving me to the pavement. Leather Pants hisses, baring his fangs. Fuck all good that'll do him. Vampires can't bite without permission. No means no, fucker.

The silly sharps still love to show their teeth. I think they get off on it, not like they can get off on anything else. Lack of blood flow is a real big drawback to not having a heartbeat.

With the vampire still hissing like a broken opossum, I draw some energy out of the air. The magic out here tastes like sadness. I focus the energy into my fist. From my back, I give my best magic-charged uppercut, hoping the punch has some kind of effect.

My fist connects with the vampire's open jaw. His mouth snaps closed. A burst of powdered teeth erupts from the sharp's mouth as his weight lifts off me. The punch knocks Leather Pants into the air. He lands on his back two feet away. I dunno if he's dead, but the gallon of blood pouring out of his mouth can't be a good sign for him.

One down.

Mohawk charges me from a crouch. She does this weird crab-walk charge. I roll and push off the ground to get on my feet. Drawing my leg back, I try to punt the damn sharp's head, but she catches my leg before the kick has any gusto. Mohawk twists and drives forward. Tendons in my right knee pop and scream as something breaks.

That's going to be a later kind of problem.

Apparently learning from Leather Pant's mistakes, Mohawk doesn't waste any time with flashy shenanigans. She slashes at me. Her hand is covered in a weird iron gauntlet thing. Each finger comes to a razor point. Sharps might not be able to bite without permission, but they can still kill your ass. She swipes at my chest.

"Bite me," I say. It's a bit of a gambit, but I've got a plan, mostly.

Not only do vampires need permission to bite, once they have it, they're like a dog with a bone. Forget everything else, get that blood.

Mohawk's mouth goes wide as she dives for my throat. She's still mid-strike. I grab her wrist and shove her hand, fingers first, into her mouth. Mohawk's black eyes go wide as she swallows her hand. I hit her elbow with a palm strike, driving her clawed fingers out the back of her skull. There's a gagging screech, and then silence as she falls to the side.

I try to jump to my feet, but my right knee buckles. The pain almost drops me again, but I catch myself. Like I said, a problem for later. I right myself and find two headless vampires on the ground.

Dreadlocks hisses something and the other four vampires move our way. Ethan is still on the ground, covered. He's not moving. The air smells of blood and death. If we don't hurry, Fox's ex isn't going to make it.

So sad.

The vampires charge, all four at Fox. Looks like they've correctly identified the threat this time. I'll magic their asses to death out of necessity. Fox will gut them and enjoy it. I hobble across the parking lot to give my wife backup she probably doesn't need.

The orange blade of her Katana flashes in the moonlight. Fox swipes diagonally down and lands in a crouch. The first sharp's head falls to the ground.

I get to her side at the same time as the other three vamps. There's still magic in the air. The flavor changes. All the death in the air, it's changing the magic. The despair fades to the stench of death. I latch on to the morbid energy, draw it in. The dead call to me. I can hear their pleas. They are dead and they are hungry.

Only a thin veil separates the living from the deceased, howling now. I reach out my hand and pull back the curtain. A ripple crosses reality. Ghostly hands reach through the threshold, grabbing at two of the vampires. The sharps look confused for a moment before their faces wrench in agony. They scream as the hungry ghosts drag them through the threshold.

The sound of Fox's blade slicing through the fourth sharp's neck sounds behind me. Before I can turn, there's a tug at my back as the hand-cannon is pulled away.

"The hell."

I turn in time for the entire parking lot to light up bright as day. The shockwave from the gun blast reverberates in my chest and my ears ring with a high-pitched tone. Smoke rises from the barrel of the gun in Fox's hands.

The last sharp is still perched over the top of the werewolf. One arm raised in the air, frozen in time. Dreadlocks, no longer has dreadlocks, or a head for that matter. There's just a bloody hole between his shoulders. After one final, freeze frame moment, the body slumps to the ground.

"Ethan!" Fox sprints to the fallen wolf.

I hobble in that direction. My knee is all kinds of broken, but that's not as big an issue as the carved-up alpha.

Ethan is covered in blood and cuts. None of them are deep enough to kill. They carved sigils and runes into his body. The markings cover him from neck to navel. Staring at them now, I see a familiar pattern. It's not the exact markings I saw in Bartholomew's vision of my parents, but it's a lot of the same symbols.

The images of the matching carvings on Ethan and my parents flash in my mind. Carvings Lloyd Burgess paid Bartholomew to etch into their skin. The old man took their lives to save his dying wife. A wife who now looks like a teenage girl and shares half my soul.

Of course, it was sharp anti-magic that got my immortal parents killed. I should have killed these fuckers slower.

Fox cradles Ethan to her chest. He looks like a giant compared to her, but she doesn't care.

Tires screech and five sets of headlights light up the night.

This better not be more sharps.

I draw on the magic. There's even more death in the air now. Maybe I can pull the curtain wide open and let some pissed off ghosts do all the work.

Three trucks, a van, and an all too familiar 1967 Mustang surround us. A whole pack of over-protective werewolves pile out, a handful already half-changed and ready to fight.

"Hey guys," I say. "You brought my car back."

The wolves growl and dig their claws into the pavement.

Chapter 3

The angry pack of wolves surrounds us, all bared teeth and vicious drool. Apparently, holding the half-dead body of their alpha isn't exactly a peace offering. It should be. We saved his ass.

"Whoa, whoa, easy." A blonde woman pushes through a wall of grizzly-bear-sized wolves. Elsa looks down at Fox. "What happened here?"

When Fox and I showed up in Hair Nation looking for guns, Elsa and a couple others kept me company while Fox made a deal with Ethan. She seemed like good people and considering she's holding back a rabid pack of dogs, she's my best-fucking-friend right this moment.

"The vampires attacked him," Fox says.

"Why would they do that?" a male voice says. He stands next to Elsa, but a full foot taller. He's got close-cropped red hair and an air of let-me-prove-myself-as-a-loyal-pup-for-the-alpha about him. His hand keeps twitching toward the stupidly large gun on his hip.

"We can tell you about it in the car," Fox says. "Right now, he needs medical attention."

"Werewolves can heal themselves, woman. He's survived worse than this."

My jaw clenches. This kid, I don't care if he is thirty, he's still an insolent child, is going to get his block knocked off if he doesn't watch how he speaks to my wife. When Elsa showed up, I'd let go of the power I'd been drawing from the air but find myself storing up once again. I took out a small hive of sharps, no damn hair is going to kill my ass ever again.

"No," Fox snaps. He green eyes glow fierce in the headlights pointed at her. "He hasn't. Look, pup. He's not healing."

If there's something an ambitious beta male hates more than being called a pup, I haven't found it. Good on Fox. Fuck that guy.

The pup growls from his chest. His shoulders bunch up, but Elsa lays a calming hand on him. His body loosens, but the narrow-eyed look of hatred doesn't fade. It would appear Elsa outranks him. The pup has no idea how lucky that makes him.

"She's right," Elsa says. "Look."

Normally, hairs heal faster than a well-trained dog begging for a treat, but something's wrong. The cuts are mostly superficial, but Ethan isn't healing. Blood seeps from the wounds and he hasn't regained consciousness. That's not normal. A couple years back, Ethan charged at me, mad that I may have accidentally got him sent to prison. I put a bullet from my .38 special through his shoulder and the hole was closed before the werewolf finished snapping my neck.

No.

This is definitely not normal.

"Get him in the van," Elsa's voice is calm, but firm. She doesn't have to shout for her pack to go into full on rescue mode.

The wolves shift back to human form. Two, now naked, men take Ethan from Fox's arms and carry him toward the van. The pack loads up in their vehicles to make the trek back to Hair Nation.

"What about them?" Pup demands.

"What about them?" Elsa says.

"They need to answer for what they did."

Okay, I've officially had enough. "What we did," I say, "is save your Alpha's ass just now. He'd be a throw rug in Vlad's den right now if we hadn't step in."

Pup's hands clench into fists. He takes a step in my direction. Let's go, kid.

Elsa steps in front of pup and sets a hand on his chest. "If Fox says she came to help, I believe her."

Pup opens his mouth, not even close to done fighting.

"But," Elsa says over top of him, "I do have a couple of questions about what happened. Fox, Sam would you be so kind as to come up to our den and fill me in on tonight's events?"

Before I can tell her I'm not going anywhere within ten miles of the worked-up beta, Fox says, "That's fine. I'd like to see that Ethan gets patched up okay anyway. If you don't mind."

"You're always welcome with us," Elsa says.

Pup growls more. Someone really needs to get this guy a lozenge. If he tries any harder to intimidate me, he's going to cough up a lung.

"I'm riding with them," Pup barks.

"Fu—" I start, but Elsa stops me with a stern look.

"I've known Fox for some time now, Jaxon. She and her husband would probably much prefer my company. You go tell Gabriel to hurry up and get Ethan up the hill. I want you to call Alice and tell her Ethan's been injured and to start working on everything she's got to fix him up. Understood?"

Jaxon glares at me.

"Jaxon, now." Elsa's voice is stern. It's a command and if werewolves are big on anything, well, it's like steak dinners, then deer piss, then guns…Chain of command is an easy top ten, though.

Jackson grunts and turns his back on us.

With the pack taking up the parking lot, the magic in the air has changed again. I prod at it in my mind. The decaying stench from earlier is gone, replaced with a pungent reek of wet dog. That I can work with. I syphon off a touch of the canine energy. The spell doesn't take much, but I throw a little wink at Jaxon's back. If Elsa catches me, she'll probably kick my ass, but screw that kid.

Three steps away, Jaxon pauses, scratches behind his ear. He looks at his hand, finds nothing, and keeps walking. Another four steps and he pauses to scratch again.

I turn my head to hide my grin and find myself face-to-face with my wife. She does not appear amused by my newfound magic skills. Jaxon stops and scratches again.

Fox sighs. "Goddammit." As she turns her head, I catch a glimpse of a smile on her beautiful lips.

"What?" Elsa asks.

Apparently, I managed to sneak the spell by her, at least.

"Nothing," Fox says. "Let's go."

Chapter 4

I gingerly take a step toward our stolen SUV, expecting my knee to be fucked from the fight. The first step is easy, no pain. Huh. In the fight, I swear I felt something snap. I take another test step, no pain. Weird. Maybe I tweaked it.

"You good?" Fox asks.

"Yeah," I say, surprised. "I guess I am."

Elsa, Fox, and I load into the SUV we stole from Sarah. I take the driver's seat and start the car. We follow the chain of cars up the mountain. Three cars up I see the taillights of my old mustang. Fox busted a couple of Hair kids out of lockup and gave them my car for a getaway ride. I'm going to be getting that back. Nothing makes a car truly your own like dying inside it a half-dozen times.

We ride in silence for a couple miles before Elsa says, "So what in God's name happened back there?"

Fox turns in her seat so she can see Elsa. After a moment, she says, "We were on our way...out of town and saw the light. When he gave me this one," Fox shows the clicker from her pocket, "he said there was only one more in existence and it was his. I know Ethan wouldn't sound the alarm unless it was bad, real bad. We were close so we came to help."

I watch Elsa in the rearview as she thinks on this.

"How did they get the drop on him? Were there a lot of them? I counted six bodies, but thought I smelled two, maybe three more."

Damn good sniffer, lady. The fight flashes back in my mind. Did I really part the veil between the living and the dead? Sarah wasn't kidding when we made our pact, intertwining my soul of immortal life and hers of necromantic death. I just pulled off some boss level magic without any real effort. There weren't even any repercussions. I feel great.

"Sam," Fox say from three states away.

"Sam." Her voice is louder and quieter all at the same time. That's weird.

Hey. Why can't I see anything?

From the next room over, tires squeal. My body bounces against the driver's door, head cracking the window glass.

"Ow," I say, holding my hand to my head.

I blink my eyes clear to find Fox reached across the car, steering from the passenger seat. The engine is redlined, my foot planted on the floorboard. Shit. I let off the accelerator and ease on the brake. With my head clear, I take the wheel and pull onto the shoulder.

"I think you might need to drive for a second," I say. "I'm not feeling so great."

"You think?" Fox says, mad. Her eyes bore into mine for a blink before she softens. "Are you okay?"

"Yeah, yeah. Dandy. Just need a nap." It's not exactly a lie. I don't remember the last time I slept, but more than that I'm the kind of tired you feel in your soul. Putting the car in park, I walk around to the passenger door.

Fox climbs across the center console and into the driver's seat. "We good?" she asks as I take my seat.

"Yeah," I say. "Follow that pack!" I point up the road and then lean my seat as far back as it goes.

The SUV spins the tires as Fox pulls back onto the road, little rocks ping across the quarter panels. Back on pavement, I can feel Fox eyeing me, but I'm too tired to look. She takes my left hand in hers. The warmth feels nice and a kind of peace rolls over me. I glance down to see Sune on the back of Fox's hand, sniffing at me.

Fox and Elsa continue their conversation at a low volume. I drift in and out as the steady rumble of the road puts me half to sleep. Every once in a while, a pothole jars me awake, but it doesn't matter. I'm beat. About the time I fall good and asleep, that best-sleep-you-can-get-in-a-moving-car kind of sleep, the tires hit gravel and skid to a stop.

Great.

We're here. Hair Nation. The pack's den, otherwise known as a warehouse full of guns with a few cottages spread around it for the wolves. The hairs are the premier arms dealers in all of Mountain City and what do they do with all that cash? Make their neighborhood look like a tiny house campground.

Elsa climbs out of the back seat. I crack an eye at Fox. If I'm lucky, she explained everything to Elsa and we're good and she can put the car in reverse and back our asses all the way to the beach. Fox gives me a gentle smile and then pushes out of the SUV.

It was worth a shot.

I can't stifle the groan as I push myself out of the car. This magic shit is a drag. I've had ass beatings that felt better than this. My body feels like it's responding in slow motion. The world around me is moving at full speed as I wade through quicksand. Next time we get attacked, I'm shooting everybody. This isn't worth it.

The caravan must have beat us here by a couple minutes. The engines are still clicking and humming from having been run hard, but they are all off and there's only one person still in the warehouse parking lot.

As we approach, the figure scratches at the back of his ear and cusses under his breath.

Fine, I lied. Some magic might be worth the cost.

"I wasn't sure you'd show," Jaxon says. He hooks his thumbs through belt loops.

"Right," Fox says. "We saved your alpha, and then we were going to run off with your pack's second in command." Fox is sure to put a little extra on 'command'.

Jaxon growls some more. Seriously, when are the hairs going to get some more original intimidation techniques? It's all growling and glowing eyes. We get it.

A day ago, a pissed off wolf wanting to pounce would have given me pause, but I'm feeling this extra power. This is great. I'm not scared of anything.

Fox's hand drifts to the katana at her side. She doesn't unsheathe the weapon, just traces her thumb across the hilt. Sune skitters up to Fox's neck and sticks her tongue out at the pup.

Elsa steps in the middle. "Enough. Both of you. Jaxon, is Ethan with the healers?"

"Yeah." Jaxon clears his throat. "Yes." His right hand twitches and starts toward his head. With a visible effort, he fights the scratch. Hard to look tuff when you're fighting a mean case of fleas.

"Good. Go and get the council. We are having a meeting in fifteen minutes. On your way back through, stop and tell the healers to send someone with a status update on Ethan's condition to the board room in thirty minutes."

"Yes, ma'am." Jaxon kicks up dust as he jogs toward the warehouse. Ten feet away, he claws at the back of his head.

Sune silently cackles on Fox's neck. The animal has both paws wrapped around its stomach from laughter.

"You two, with me." Elsa walks toward the biggest of the cottages without waiting to see if we follow.

Fox follows without hesitation, and I follow my wife, with great hesitation. My head is still foggy from…exertion? When I studied magic before, I remember reading about how heavy-duty spells can take a lot out of the caster, but it took me fifty years to learn how to make a big enough fire to light a cigarette. Small time magic meant small time consequences. I'm guessing messing with the fabric separating the spirit world counts as slightly more than small time. There's going to be a wicked hangover for this tomorrow, no doubt.

I jog a couple steps so I'm next to Fox.

"You alright?" she asks under her breath.

Elsa can probably hear us, canine senses and all, but she keeps walking with her head held high.

"I've been better."

Fox takes my hand again. A warmth passes through my chest like I'm some kind of school kid. I've been around this world a long time and here I am, still butterflies and dopey grins for this woman. I've heard all the love songs of the ages, read more than a few books about it, but never in my life until now did I understand what it felt like.

The three of us walk to the nicest of the cabins. This one is two floors, with a cozy second story balcony looking out over the compound. The front of the house is all glass, bright lights inside reach out into the night.

"Is this what I think it is?" I ask.

"Ethan's house," Fox says.

Of course, Fox knows this, they dated before we met. A hired killer broke in and tried to kill Fox and Ethan over some bad business. Fox told me she'd wanted to break up with Ethan. Breaking up with an alpha is like breaking up with your left arm, if your left arm had big teeth and a bigger possessive complex. The hitmen cut up Fox real bad. Sune hitched a ride out on one of the attackers and left Ethan to think she was dead. A clean break. Ethan knew Fox to be dead up until we showed up at his house two nights ago looking for a favor.

Elsa opens the door and invites the three of us inside. I pause at the threshold. It feels weird walking into an alpha's house. They get territorial and he already thinks I stole his girl. If he thinks it was anything other than her stealing me, he clearly didn't know Fox.

"It's okay," Elsa says, apparently sensing my feelings. "I have the authority to speak on Ethan's behalf. You are welcome in this home for now."

The 'for now' of that statement is not lost on me. I'm guessing it extends up to point-oh-one seconds after the alpha wakes up. No point in arguing, I plan to be long gone by then.

The inside of the small house is a wide-open floor plan. Living room, dining room, and kitchen. The whole house is exquisite looking wood, except for the granite and stainless steel in the kitchen.

The refrigerator is some kind of custom job, the biggest thing I've ever seen. A set of stairs leads to a loft. From the first floor I can see the foot of a huge bed, but don't spend too long looking.

"I kind of expected bigger." I have no idea why I said that. As if I can judge this beautiful cabin in the woods when I live in a one room roach motel in the Glow. The bag of cash in the SUV speaks to me. That's not our apartment anymore. We've got cash. With these new powers, I'm sure I can find a way to make more if needed.

"Ethan doesn't spend much time here," Fox says. "From the time he wakes up until bed he's out there working. Either in the warehouse, or in the office, or out doing TV stuff to try and repair the Hair image damaged by Old Man Bugess."

Lloyd Burgess, the husband or maybe ex-husband, of Sarah is a standard who runs the city. The old fuck probably has enough money that God asks him for stock tips. Burgess has had it out for the hairs for a long time. He's been waging war against them in the news and in the streets. Ethan has been fighting back though. He's well-spoken, good looking, and passionate. The kind of guy any girl would…I'm going to stop thinking now.

Elsa motions toward the dining room table. The thing must be ten foot long with a half-dozen chairs on each side and one more at each end.

"Have a seat," Elsa says. "The council will be starting shortly."

Chapter 5

I stare at the woodgrain of the table, waiting on a bunch of angry hairs to come in and blame me. My body aches from the magic and I can already feel the migraine that's waiting for me. As I sit and try to relax, I can't stop seeing Ethan all cut up from the sharps.

Sharps can heal from all wounds but one, sunlight. The sun causes thick burns, like a brand, that never leave their skin. The sharps got to placing stencils on their skin and burning themselves on purpose, etching the markings into their bodies for all eternity. It's fucked up, but whatever works.

The shapes and symbols all look like gibberish to me. The sharps aren't much for people who don't have fangs. With a few exceptions for P.I. work, I've avoided the sharps and their anti-magic ways. Thinking on the stuff carved in Ethan's chest, though. It's familiar.

My hands clench into fists as it dawns on me. I've seen the carvings on my parents' bodies. I got a glimpse of what happened to them when their immortality was stripped away. The magic, or anti-magic, came from the sharps.

Fox sets her hand on mine. "Are you okay?"

This is not the time or the place to talk this out. "Yeah," I say. "Just a muscle spasm from the magic back there. I'll be fine after a nap, and maybe a post nap romp."

"A post nap romp? Are you hitting on the queen of England?"

"Only if it's working on the queen sitting next to me." Fox grins as a group of eight wolves enter the room.

Jaxon is first, followed by Gabriel. I met Gabriel with Elsa the other night. They both seemed alright. The other six, three men and three women, I don't know. A couple of them offer smiles to Fox, a couple more seem pissed at our presence. Jaxon, head among them.

"What are they doing here?" Jaxon points. "This is pack business."

"They saved our pack leader's life. They are here for this one discussion only." Elsa spreads her arms. "Everyone, take a seat."

Elsa sits at the head of the table, temporary shot caller.

There are a few murmurs among the group as they take their seats. I could hear the words if I were paying attention, but I don't care. They can think what they want. I just want to go home.

Jaxon stomps across to the kitchen, grabs a jug of deer piss out of a cabinet, and stomps back to the table. He takes a seat opposite Elsa, chugs a quart of the alcohol in one go, and slams the glass down on the table. Deer piss is every hair's favorite drink. I had some the other night. It's enough to strip the paint off a car clear down to the frame, but it tastes slightly better than the name suggests. Kind of like pure fire, with a smoked oak finish.

"As you all have heard, a group of sharps attacked Ethan tonight," Elsa says. Her posture is straight, but the large chair seems to make her small. She tucks a strand of platinum blonde hair behind her ear. "He's alive, but they did something to him. His body isn't healing like it should."

A small round of whispers before Gabriel says, "How is that even possible?"

"I don't know." Elsa takes a look around the table. "We know the sharps have developed wards against magic, maybe they have something against us as well. The brand is known to all already."

The brand is an image of a wolf eating its tail. If the image is applied to a hair's skin, it prevents the hair from shifting into their wolf form. It's generally applied by brand, but I've seen it carved by knife as well. The wolves healing ability usually closes the wound within an hour or two, restoring their abilities.

"So what," a man with long black hair and brown skin says, "you think they were testing new tech? Seeing what would happen?"

"Vampires are crazy fuckers," I say. Hell, why did I speak? No point in stopping now. "But they aren't stupid. They know Ethan is your alpha. If you are beta testing, starting with the baddest ass in the pack doesn't seem like a good move."

"You're saying he was targeted?" the man asks.

"What the hell does this Standard even know?" Jaxon throws his arms up, takes another swig of juice, and scratches behind his ear.

"He's not a standard," Fox says. Her voice is loud and confident, exuding authority. Sune is standing neatly on her neck, getting a view of the whole table. "Sam has been around a long time, longer than any of you. He knows what he's talking about."

"Why is she even here?" This from a blonde with a Russian accent.

Weird, but okay. They've got hairs from all over, come to join the Mountain City circus.

"After what she did to alpha," the Russian continues, "we should kill her and feed her to the pups."

Jaxon slaps his hand on the table. "Yeah," he screams. "That's what I'm talking about."

Elsa silences them both with a stare.

Jaxon flinches under her gaze and slumps in his chair. The Russian doesn't kowtow quite as much, but she shuts her mouth all the same.

"Ethan cared deeply for Fox," Elsa says. "And she saved his life. Do you really want to guess how he's going to feel when he finds out you disrespected her, Anna? Or any of you for that matter? Fox and Sam are my guests, here on my invitation. Any slight against either of them, is a slight against me. Understood?"

A silent round of nods from the table. Gabriel holds a hand up to his face, but I can see the smile underneath. If I didn't know any better, I'd say he likes seeing the kids put into line.

"Since you offered your expert opinion, Mr. Flint, what do you think happened?" Jaxon asks.

That's a great question. It'd be even better if I had a great answer. "To be perfectly honest? I don't know. It seems highly unlikely that your alpha gets carved up by accident or unfortunate happenstance. I'd put money it was intentional. The sharps been messing with you all any?"

"There have been some recent…incursions," the black-haired man says. "We wrote it off as young sharps testing the boundaries, but there has been an uptick in sharps on our side of the line."

"You think Darius is up to something?" Gabriel asks.

"Darius has never had a problem with us before," Black-Hair says. "Why would he start up now?"

Darius is the closest thing the sharps have to a leader. They don't have the hierarchy down quite like the hairs, but Darius was old when I was a kid. Old ass beings generally don't start shit for no reason, but this is on the hairs to figure out. I never should have spoken up. I'm not their P.I. and I wouldn't be even if they asked me.

"Sam, do you think Burgess could have been behind this?" Elsa's gaze is pointed directly at me.

This doesn't feel like Burgess. He's got the cops of Mountain City in his back pocket and has been waging a smear campaign against the hairs for years now. Burgess also employs the most powerful mages in the city. I'm not sure he'd send a sharpie hit squad that couldn't even get the job done.

"I don't know." It's not a lie. There is a definite connection between Burgess and the sharps, but something feels off.

"This standard doesn't know a—" Jaxon catches a glimpse of Elsa and clears his throat. "With all due respect, I have to disagree with Flint. This is a direct attack on the pack. No one has more against us than Burgess."

"And besides," Anna growls with a face that says she enjoys saying the words as little as the rest of us enjoy hearing them, "isn't Mr. Flint employed by the old man? He might have a, how you say, conflict of interest."

A pack of hair representatives stare my way.

"Was employed. I finished the job and was on my way out of town when we saw your boss getting attacked. Trust me when I say, I want as little to do with Burgess as you."

"I doubt that." Anna checks the crimson paint on her fingernails, already bored with the conversation.

"Doubt whatever you want. I'm leaving."

Fox sets a hand on my leg a split-second before I bolt from my chair. We did these guys a favor and they're over here giving us the third degree.

"They helped my boy." The voice belongs to a man. His brown eyes stare at Fox and I. "Sean got picked up on some standard bullshit. He said Fox did something to the guards, broke him out, and gave him her car to get back here."

A car I'm going to be needing back.

"You're not the only one, Thomas," a woman says. Her gray hair is pulled back in a gentle braid. Soft lines on her face show a lifetime of happiness. "Lance and his cousin Jebediah got arrested over a scrap. The boys said some guy and his red-haired wife sent in a shark of a lawyer. She had them out before the ink was dry on the arrest."

"So what, Thomas, Marguerite," Jaxon says, "you think these two are honorary pack members now? For all we know they've got the cops on their payroll."

I can't stop the laugh that bursts out of my chest. "We live in the Glow. And not in that rich kids slumming it kind of thing. Our one room apartment in the shittiest part of town is what we can afford."

Well, if you don't count the pile of cash in the backseat of our ride.

"So yeah, I'm paying the cops off with what, exactly? My rugged good looks?"

The door opens and a young girl, maybe eight or nine, steps in. She caught me mid-bitching and is frozen in place.

"It's okay, Shel," Elsa says. "You can come in." Elsa's voice is gentle, soothing. The way she can go from shutting down Jaxon to calming a child is impressive. No wonder she's Ethan's right hand.

"Ummm..." Shel's eyes dart around, taking in all the people.

"Don't worry," Elsa says. "You can talk in front of us. We just want to know how Ethan is doing."

Shel wraps her arms behind her back, grabbing elbows with opposite hands. "Momma says it's…weird. Said she hasn't seen anything like it before. Ethan's not healing like he should. Momma's working on some roots and stuff, but she said she's mostly trying to make him comfortable. He's stable, she thinks?"

"She thinks?" Jaxon's voice is a bark, sending the little girl a step toward the door.

Elsa's nails dig into the wood of the table as she bores a hole through Jaxon with her eyes.

"Why did she not tell us herself?" Anna asks.

"Oh, um. She said she was afraid to leave Ethan's side. So she asked me to come."

"Thank you, Shel," Elsa says. "Did she say anything else?"

Shel shakes her head and looks at the floor.

"Very well. Go back to your mother. Tell her to come to me if she needs anything, anything at all."

The little girl is out the room in a blink.

"I think we've gotten as much as we can for the night. Sam, Fox, the pack thanks you for what you did tonight. If we can ever repay you, don't hesitate to ask." Elsa turns her attention to the rest of the table. "Everyone else, I want increased perimeter security, twenty four-seven surveillance. Work amongst yourself to figure out the schedule. Does anyone have any questions?"

The cutting tone in Elsa's voice tells everyone there will be no questions.

The pack picks up on it, hairs are good at that. They all give silent nods.

"Good. Everyone get some rest. Tomorrow morning I'll have another update on Ethan and we can figure out how to go forward if he is still incapacitated."

The council all stand up and head for the door. Jaxon makes sure he's the last to leave to buy an extra thirty second to glare at me between scratches. The last scratch as he heads out the door, I catch a glimpse of blood on his fingertips.

A heavy hand lands on my shoulder. "You've had your fun," Elsa says. "Fix him."

Damn. She did catch me, and she just let it happen. Elsa must like Jaxon less than I do to let an outsider fuck with a pack member.

I focus on the back of Jaxon's head. A small glow behind his ear shows my spell. I blow a stiff breath of air and the blue glow releases into the wind. Magic dissolves back into the air for future use.

"Thank you," Elsa says. "It's late and you two look like hell."

With the roller coaster of sharps and hairs, I hadn't thought about my looks. I check my body, not a scratch on my skin but sharp blood covers my clothes. Fox is cleaner, but there's still spatters of crimson across her shirt. My dried blood coats her sneakers from where Sarah's mage goons repeatedly killed me.

"We have a guest house. Would you like to use it?"

Good question, forty-five minute drive back to our apartment or comfy cabin surrounded by animals who want to eat me. It's a real conundrum.

"I think we'd be more comfortable at our place tonight," Fox says.

Thank god.

"But would you mind if we stop by tomorrow afternoon to check on Ethan?"

Goddammit.

Elsa smiles at Fox. "I think Ethan would very much appreciate that."

"Thank you." Fox wraps an arm around me and pulls me toward the door.

"Hey," I say. "About my car?"

Elsa smiles. "Sean is going to be heartbroken, but yes. I don't blame you for wanting it back. The keys should be in it."

"You all leave the keys in the car?"

"We are in the middle of Hair Nation, surrounded by pack and guns." Elsa shrugs. "Who would be stupid enough to steal from this place?"

I can think of a handful of people dumb enough off the top of my head, but I'm tired. "Tell the kid he can have a Cadillac as a consolation prize. I probably wouldn't suggest driving it downtown. It's not exactly registered.

Elsa laughs. "I'm sure the boys can find a way to have some fun in the Nation."

I jog over to the SUV and grab the leather bag full of cash, Fox's sword, and the magic handgun. Down to four bullets. The shit better not hit the fan before I can figure out how to get more rounds for that thing.

I reach for the driver's door, but Fox pushes it closed.

"After that stunt on the way up here, I think I'll do the driving."

"You just want some more time behind the wheel of this beast."

"Ever heard of killing two birds with one stone? I'm keeping you safe and stretching the old pony's legs." Fox pushes me out of the way with her hip and slides behind the wheel.

Damn, that's sexy.

I toss the money and weapons into the back seat as I slide into the passenger side.

As promised, the keys are waiting in the ignition. Fox presses the clutch and twists the key. The engine roars to life and settles into a lumpy burble. The side mirror shakes in time to the engine.

Elsa leans into the driver's window. "I'm sorry about the way some of the pack were acting, but believe me. I understand what you did tonight. Our pack appreciates it more than we can express. We are strong, but Ethan is the alpha for a reason. I'm not sure what we'd do without him."

"Are you kidding?" Fox asks. "I saw you in there. You're one badass bitch."

Elsa flashes a toothy grin. She pats the roof of the car. "You two go get some sleep. And a shower. You smell like death."

Chapter 6

The air smells of burnt rubber as Fox hauls out of Hair Nation at record speed. The smile on her face stretches ear-to-ear. She doesn't speak the entire way down the hill, just enjoys the speed. The entire pack is huddled around their alpha and no cop would be caught dead in hair territory. The road is hers and she takes up every inch of it, using the mountain like her own personal touge course.

The moment we cross out of hairitory and into downtown, Fox jams the shifter into fourth and lets her foot off the throttle. The engine smooths from a scream to a steady rumble as the car eases into cruising speed. Cops are always thick at the borders. Everyone stay in your little corner of the city, don't bring any bullshit downtown. It's where all the standards act like they aren't as crooked as every other creature in town.

"So," Fox says, "back there with the sharps…"

"Yeah?"

"I'm not gonna lie, it looked an awful lot like ghosts appeared and snatched two fangers straight out of reality."

"Oh yeah, that."

"That," Fox repeats.

"I'm not sure how I did that, exactly."

Fox watches me out of the corner of her eye. "But you're saying you did do that? It wasn't some cosmic glitch with great timing?"

"Nope. Just your husband who sold his soul to the devil, but still has great timing."

"Cute."

I set a hand on Fox's thigh. Sune tracks down Fox's body to her leg. The tattoo sniffs at my hand, like it's expecting to find something different about me. Apparently satisfied, Sune curls up into a ball underneath my palm and goes to sleep.

"So that episode in the car?"

"Apparently, with great magic comes great tendencies to pass out. Someone should have warned me. Do not drive or operate heavy machinery after fucking with reality."

Fox huffs out a laugh. "How do you feel now?"

"I'm pretty beat, but in the last twenty-four hours I've died like four times and fought a small swarm of sharps. There's a solid chance I'm just tired."

"Good point. Listen, I want to get to the beach as much as you, but--"

"But we need to get some sleep first."

"Yes. We do." Fox sounds relieved.

She knows how much I want out of this place. This town has brought me nothing but misery for all my lives. I tried to end it all but then I met Fox. She's the only good thing that's come out of this cesspool of a town.

"We can get cleaned up and some sleep," I say. "Tomorrow we'll go check on Ethan and then hit the road. It's not like I've got to work tomorrow, or ever again. So, there's no rush. We're on beach time, babe. We'll get there when we get there."

"Wow." Fox takes her eyes off the road to look dead at me. "That's a very mature response."

"I'm very mature."

"You're very old. That doesn't mean mature."

"Touché."

The rest of the ride home is quiet. We're both tired and by the time we make it home to our apartment, neither of us has the energy to do anything more than pass out in each other's arms.

######

Sun shines on the side of my face. The warm heat wakes me from something closer to death than sleep. I don't know if we've been asleep for hours or days, but I feel like a brand-new man. Maybe this magic shit ain't so tiring. Who knows, last night I could have been tired from sleep deprivation and I'm actually so good at magic now that I don't even get tired. Yeah. Let's go with that.

I crack an eye to find Fox snuggled up against my side. Neither of us so much as took our shoes off before passing out last night. Our sheets are covered in dirt and sharp blood. Doesn't matter. We are leaving this place today and never looking back.

The covers don't matter, but being covered in bloody clothes isn't my favorite. I slide out from under Fox. She groans in her sleep and quickly replaces her favorite husband with her favorite pillow. I can't even pretend to be offended. It's a fair trade.

I strip off my clothes and grab the most glorious shower I've had in this life. So, what if this life is less than twenty-four hours old? It's still one hell of a shower.

Once I've sufficiently cleaned the dead off, I dry myself with an old towel and get dressed.

"Hey, babe," I say, gently. "It's time to wake up."

Fox groans but doesn't move.

Come on, lady. We've got to get this show on the road. I know I said we're on beach time, but I take it back. Beach time starts when I can hear seagulls. Now we're on 'get the hell out of here' time.

I reach out to shake Fox just as a knock sounds at the door. Who the hell?

Fox's eyes snap open. She spins into a kneeling position on the bed. Somehow there is a stiletto blade in her right hand. One day she's going to have to show me where she hides all these blades.

"Easy. It's probably the landlord. Have we paid rent this year?"

Fox shrugs. Her eyes are locked on the door, knuckles white under tension.

I walk across the room and open the door expecting to see our twitchy-ass standard landlord, or the twitchy-ass hair tweaker who lives next door, or the twitchy-ass old woman who lives at the end of the hall. What I don't expect to see is a five-foot tall woman in her late 30s. A blue and gold kimono wraps her body. She stares up at me with the kind of haughty disinterest of a queen when asked what she thinks of the plight of the working man.

Two bodyguards stand behind her, both with hands crossed in front of their belts. Each man is nearly a foot taller than the old woman. They both sport katanas and their draw of magical energy does not escape me. These guys are not messing around.

"Can I help you?"

It's a dumb question. Clearly, I can't help them. They are obviously looking for a royal dry cleaning company in the middle of the Glow?

The woman's heavily made-up face curls at my words. "No. Move to the side so I can take my daughter home." She leans around me to peer at Fox in bed. "Mariko, it's been long enough. Time to come home."

"Mom?" Fox sounds confused, but not near as confused as I am.

Chapter 7

"Wait. You name's not Fox?" I ask, still half-stunned by the little woman claiming to be Fox's mother.

"Yes," Fox snaps. "It is."

Oh, okay, cool then. Clears that right up.

The woman pushes past me, her two bodyguards following.

"Mariko," the woman's voice is stern, harsh, "I've come all this way to get you. Tracked you to this…" The woman examines our apartment. "This filth. You ran away from the palace. I have been more than patient. Your time is up. You will come home and fulfill your royal duties."

Did she say palace? Royal what now? I have so, so many questions. Fox and I made an agreement when we married, we would never ask about each other's past. We've both lived more than a few lifetimes and we both have plenty of shit buried that doesn't need to come back. Being royalty, though, that might warrant a small discussion. This is not the time or the place. I can ask about it after these shit stains leave my wife alone.

Fox is still crouched on the bed, death grip on the blade in her hand. Whatever this lady, her mom, wants, my wife is not open to the idea.

"No." That's it, Fox's only response. No diatribe, no reasoning, just one solid, resounding no.

The word hangs in the air.

The two samurai mages suck up more power. This is my home, my magic to take. I sneak some quick sips of magic, topping off the tank. Here, in my bedroom, the magic tastes like cigarettes and sex and coffee and love.

"Mariko," the old woman snaps. "This is not up for debate. I have prepared a suitable vessel for your return trip home. A young woman of more desirable lineage awaits the honor of giving her body to you. You shall not make her wait for the honor of ascendance. You will leave this life of squalor and come back to the royal grounds."

Fox doesn't respond.

Her mom scoffs. "You should be home, being worshipped as the goddess you are. Instead, you are here being—"

"Worshipped like the goddess she is," I say. I've had enough of this old broad talking shit about our life. "Do you give one single damn that your daughter is happy?"

"Silence, boy. No one addressed you." The woman whips a hand in my direction.

A gale force wind shoves me against kitchen cabinets. My elbow goes through the wood front and crashes into my favorite coffee cups. Splintered wood and porcelain fall down my shoulders.

So, it wasn't only the guards. The woman knows her way around magic as well. On the back of her hand, I notice a familiar figure. A fox swirls and silently yips on the back of her hand. The fox has a similar look as my wife's, but it's different. The animal has five or six tails, where Sune only has one. I wonder if Sune can get more tails. How many tails can she get? Is six the max or is there a ten tails out there? Can Fox do magic too? More questions to file away for later.

"Mariko, let's go."

Fox's eyes dart to me, still pinned against my own kitchen wall. "No," she says, softer this time.

Oh, hell no. Fox has watched my half-defenseless ass get killed over and over. I've stranded her with trolls and zombies and all kind of other evil while I rematerialized fifty miles away. Not today. Not ever again.

I had been sipping at the energy in the air, but I open up the dam. Not only does the latent power in the air fill my soul, I feel myself draining it away from the other mages. Strongest dog eats first.

The whirlwind pinning me to the wall dies, no energy left to blow my walls down. I step toward my mother-in-law and her guards. They watch me with a wide-eyed apprehension that wasn't there before. Both guards grip their swords.

"She said she didn't want to go with you," I say. The words come straight from my chest, bubbling up with the magic that's ready to burst from every pore of my being.

"This does not concern you," the old woman says.

"Yes. It does." I take a step forward. Focusing my power on the trio, I used my mind and push them.

All three lift an inch off the ground before floating toward the door. They try to outdraw me. Not here, not now. This is my house. Both men attempt to draw their swords as they reach the threshold of my door. I imagine steel shattering. The men draw swords with no blades, only grips.

With a visible heave, the two mages suck enough power to break my spell. All three touch down on the ground. The woman steps back toward the hall. The two guards stand in front of her. Their focus is solely on me.

Idiots.

They step forward in unison. I still have a huge well of magic and I start thinking about that curtain from last night. There was a lot of death in the air then, the magic practically begged for necromancy. The magic here is different, but I might be able to make it work.

I think about the other side and focus my energy. The ghost of a sharp appears in the corner of the room. The sharp doesn't have any of the anti-magic markings of his race. Even as a spectral image of a man, I can see the left half of his body covered in burn. It doesn't look like what killed him, but it can't have been pleasant either. The ghost hisses and crawls toward the samurai on hands and knees.

No one else acknowledges the ghost in the room. They might not be able to see it.

As the ghost crawls hand over foot toward the mercs, the phantom image shatters as Fox steps through its head. She dives at the guard closest to her, driving the stiletto blade into the side of his neck. The guard thrashes but he's not reaching for the blade. Instead, he grabs a handful of Fox's red hair and flips her over his shoulder.

Fox does her best to roll with the judo throw, but our apartment is too small. She crashes into me, knocking both of us over backward.

The guards waste no time in getting to work. Samurai Bob tears the knife from his neck and tosses it to the ground like a toy. Blood spews from the wound for a blink before skin heals over the puncture.

That would be a real cool trick in a bar. Less cool on my would-be assassin.

Samurai Bob grabs another handful of Fox's hair. He drags her off me kicking and cussing. Silver glints in the dim light of my apartment as Fox slashes back with another blade. Bob catches Fox's wrist and twists it behind her.

Samurai Rich seems to think Fox is contained and heads for me. He draws a short sword from the backside of his armor. I crab walk away, but there's no time to get to my feet. Rich dives at me, pushing the blade at my throat. In this type of situation, I find it's always best to worry about the thing that's going to kill you fastest. Sure, Rich can probably martial art me to death, but none of that matters if his blade leaves me headless first.

I will not die here and strand Fox, again.

I catch Samurai Rich's wrist in both my hands, pushing the sword away from my skin. The guy is strong. A small swell of energy moves through the air like a wave and suddenly Rich is pushing with the strength of a dozen men. I try to focus on a spell, but I can't concentrate with the blade creeping towards my throat.

"Hey, Sharpie, little help here?"

As if he needed an invitation, the vampire ghost leaps onto the Samurai's back.

"Nani?"

Vampire Valley

The ghost bites straight into Rich's neck. Apparently, ghost sharps don't need permission. The blade scatters across the stained linoleum floor. Exactly the opening I needed. I grab the weapon. A clean slice from my back is awkward, but the blade is sharp and true. It doesn't take perfect form to separate head from body. The samurai's dome rolls across the floor, coming to a rest in a pile of broken coffee cups.

There's still another threat. I jump to my feet to find Bob dragging Fox toward the door, one arm wrapped around her neck, the other still fighting over the blade in her hand.

This is going to take perfect timing. Fox, do you trust me? No time to ask out loud and ruin the surprise. I sprint forward. Using momentum for strength, I put both hands on Fox's wrist and drive her hand backwards. The power is too much and the butterfly knife sinks three inches deep into Bob's eyeball.

The guy doesn't so much as grunt, but he does release the hold. Fox spins away from his grip. The butterfly knife is still in Bob's eye, but Fox already has a tiny, arrowhead shaped blade drawn. The weapon has a small T-shaped grip that sits in her palm. The blade sticks out between her knuckles like the world's scariest brass knucks.

She won't need the knife. Not this time.

With the dead samurai in the room, the energy has already shifted. The air tastes of dirt and some kind of floral scent I can't place. I suck up every bit of the new magic and draw the curtain back. Three wraiths howl from the other side and attack Samurai Bob. Now he screams.

The specters tear at his armor, down to flesh in a snap. They feast on his body, on his soul.

The man screams as he swipes at the ghosts hungry for any bit of humanity they can find.

Last night, I cracked the veil and the ghosts took their meal to-go. I fucked up and opened it too far today. These ghosts are here now.

"Hey, guys," I say, "time to go home."

The ungrateful bastards ignore me. Sharpie tries to get in on the action, but he can't get a bite in edgewise. The new ghosts are spinning and clawing so fast I can't even be sure it's only three of them. I grab Fox's hand and sneak us around the frenzy.

We meet Fox's mom in the hallway. I pull the door closed. Doors keep ghosts out, right? Right. Maybe I should read a book or watch an internet video about the veil before I mess with it again. Probably a good idea.

There's a fiery look in Fox's mom's eyes, but her demeanor is calm.

"I'm not going back," Fox says.

"Marik--"

"That's *not* my name and I'm *not* going back. You have Ariko, your golden daughter. Leave me alone."

"Ariko cannot be the heir and you know why."

Fox's upper lip curls. "She's your blood. That's more than me."

"You are more precious than blood. Mariko, you are my *shippo*." The woman extends a hand toward Fox.

"Mariko is dead. Okay. Dead. There, now Ariko is the heir. I know your secret, mother. If you try to force me home, I'll tell everyone the truth behind your miracle blood child."

The woman snatches her hand away, wincing as if Fox had punched her. "You would bring dishonor upon our lineage?"

"I was not the one who brought dishonor upon your house. That was you, Hisa." Fox grabs my arm and drags me toward the stairs.

The woman doesn't give chase. "Watashi wa modorimasu," she says, as she watches the two of us leave.

Chapter 8

Fox storms through the stairwell door, down the stairs, and out into the afternoon light without a word. I follow, equal parts confused and worried. Did I marry a Japanese princess? A goddess? That would be the worst children's movie plot of all time. Angry princess leaves her homeland and marries a bum who can't quit dying.

We walk, well I walk and Fox stomps like the pavement has wronged her, across the street to the car.

Fox tears the mustang door open and slams it behind her as she drops in the driver's seat. I take my position in the passenger seat. The leather duffle is sitting in plain sight on the back seat. How tired were we last night? The last thing we need is our running away money to get jacked by some idiot kid.

"You okay?" I ask.

Fox's jaw clenches.

"Dumb question. Clearly you aren't okay," I say. "You want to talk about that?"

"Not for all the money in the world." She twists the key and the engine fires to life like an angry dragon.

The tires squeal as she pulls into traffic without so much as a glance in the rearview. We live in the middle of the Glow, named for all the neon lights of the shitholes selling drugs, more drugs, and the occasional body so they can afford drugs of their own. It's the part of town where any race who can't afford a nice house in the hills with the rest of their species live.

The streets are alive with a special kind of fuck the world. The people here are never going to get out and they know it. Some rage about it. They drink and fight and bitch about the man. Others accept their fate and try to enjoy their time drinking and fighting and bitching about the man, whoever the man may be in their particular case.

The Glow passes in a blur. As Fox tears through city, the engine screams all the words she's not. She swerves and dodges any car not smart enough to get the hell out of the way. I want to tell her to slow down, to take it easy, but it doesn't matter. If this is how she wants to burn off steam, that's fine.

My phone buzzes in my pocket. That's weird. No one calls me. I dig out the phone.

Blocked number.

Hell if I'm going to answer that.

I end the call and slide the phone back. "Probably a telemarketer."

As we come up on Downtown, Fox cuts a sharp left. The fastest way is straight through town, but there are standards galore in Downtown and where there are standards, there are cops. I'd bet that Fox is taking the long way around to avoid the MCPD's finest. That's probably best for the cops.

Fox's knuckles are white from griping the steering wheel. Every shift she punches the car into gear, popping the clutch and barking the tires.

I set a reassuring hand on her thigh. Sune paces from Fox's knee to her neck and back again. Even the tattoo is keyed up. That's not a great sign.

The hour-long drive to the limits of Hair Nation is over in forty minutes. The car smells like antifreeze and gasoline. We might need that SUV back by the end of this.

The gravel lot at the hair warehouse is full of cars today. They must have called all hands on deck. I wonder if that means Ethan is better enough to call a war council or he's not better and they're here to pay their respects. I keep the thought to myself.

I give Fox's thigh one last squeeze before we climb out of the car. Waves of heat roll off the hood. Something hisses from near the radiator.

Fox marches toward the warehouse, head high like she belongs here. It makes sense. This was her home once.

Shut the hell up, head. She chose you. Don't be a little bitch.

Gabriel and another hair I don't know stand in front of the entrance, both armed with comically large caliber rifles.

"Christ, Fox," Gabriel says. "You look like hell."

"Gabe. I want, no I *need* to put my fist through something right now. Do you really want that something to be you?"

The other hair, dude with a shaved head in his early 40s, shifts to the side. He glances from Gabriel to Fox and back. His finger keeps moving from the handle to the trigger and back.

Gabriel holds his hands up. "No, ma'am. Are you okay?"

"Fucking peachy."

Gabriel waits for more. It's not coming.

"Okay then," Gabriel says. "Are you here to see Ethan?"

"Can I?" Fox glances at me. "Can we?"

"Elsa said to run all visitors through her. I don't think she'll mind, but let me give her a call. Otherwise, you'll have to get in line to kick my ass."

Fox's veneer of fury cracks for a moment as she offers the hair a knowing smile.

Gabriel digs his phone out of his jeans pocket and clicks around on the screen. "Hey, Elsa," he says. "Fox and Sam are here and wondering if they could come up…Okay. Cool. I'll send them."

"You're good," Gabriel says. "Fox, he's up in his office."

"I remember the way."

Fox leads me inside the large warehouse. Crates upon crates of guns are stacked impossibly tall. A forklift beeps somewhere on the other side of the room. Hardhat-clad hairs rush about their day of shipping and receiving. The room smells like sawdust and gun oil.

A stairwell to the right of the door leads us up to a walkway that traces the edges of the warehouse. We walk toward the back where there's a row of small offices. Hairs pass by, some giving Fox a casual nod, others glaring at her. They can scowl all they want, but they better keep their thoughts to themselves. I don't care if Fox did break their alphas heart. Life happens. Get over it.

The middle door is the largest of the offices. Wide windows would give the occupant an excellent view of the warehouse if the shades weren't down.

Fox gives the door three gentle knocks.

The door swings open. Elsa's bloodshot eyes greet us. Did she sleep at all last night?

"You look even worse than I do," Elsa says to Fox.

"Gabriel is already on my shit list. Do I have to go and add you, too?" Fox cracks the smallest of grins.

Elsa smiles back. "Come in."

A large oak desk faces the windows. The oversized workspace sports enough room for three people. On one side, a small laptop sits covered in stacks of papers. Invoices, contracts, and who knows what else. A medium-sized television rests on the other corner. The screen shows a smug newscaster with the volume on mute.

O'Malley's dumb face furiously preaches into the cameras. Even on mute it's clear the guy is spouting the kind of hyperbole that would get him knocked unconscious in the Glow. He's not in the Glow, though, he's on network television 'reporting' on the kinds of stories that keep the standards scared and the flames of hatred well stoked.

Two days ago, Ethan appeared as a guest on O'Malley's show, trying to defend the hair population from the blatant racism coming their way. Ethan made a valiant effort, but let's be honest, people watching O'Malley Today aren't interested in having their minds changed by facts or compassion. Every bit as ravenous as the sharps out in the valley, they only want blood. It doesn't even matter whose. At least the sharps have the manners to ask permission before they drain you dry.

"Has he been like this all night?" Fox's voice draws my eyes away from the television.

Ethan is laid out across a large couch. The thing looks long enough to hold Ethan in human or werewolf form, his body eclipsed in the supple leather. The healers cleaned away all the blood, revealing the masterwork of symbols carved into his skin. The flesh hasn't scabbed over, but the cuts aren't openly bleeding either. The wounds aren't particularly deep, and it doesn't take a specialist in lycanthropy to know he should have been healed up by now.

"Yeah," Elsa says. "The healers have no idea what to do. Something about the symbols is stifling his healing ability."

Fox kneels next to the couch. She takes Ethan's hand and rubs her thumb across it. Something flares in my chest, but I swallow the emotion. I will *not* be jealous of a guy in a coma, goddammit.

I think about all the hairs down in the factory, plugging away like nothing's wrong.

"The pack doesn't know about this," I say, not a question.

"Only the ones from the council last night," Elsa says. "The pack has work to do and nothing will get done if they are worried about their alpha."

"What are you doing for him?" Fox asks. She hasn't taken her eyes off the werewolf's carved up body.

Elsa blows out a breath. "What can we do? I have the healers looking through all the old texts they can find. You know the sharps, though. They've always been secretive of their magic. If they had some kind of anti-hair tech, they probably didn't share."

My phone buzzes. I ignore it.

"There's a place down in the Glow," Fox says. "Santa Rosita's Herbs and Oddities. Have one of your people go down there. Tell them Fox sent them. Rosita knows a little bit of everything. She might be able to help."

Elsa nods. She slides over to a phone on the desk with enough buttons to launch a space shuttle. Pressing a button, she says, "Send Thomas up, please."

A clipped, "Yes, ma'am," from the speaker and Elsa releases the button.

A couple moments later, the black-haired man from last night enters the room. He glances at Ethan with a grimace. "Yes, ma'am."

"There's an herbalista down in the Glow, Santa Rosita. I want you to go down there, tell her Fox sent you, and ask if she knows anything that might help. Don't use any names, just say a pack member was attacked by sharps."

Thomas gives a slight bow to Elsa and sees himself out of the room.

As the door closes, I catch a ripple in the air to my right. I turn in time to see a pale, teenage girl with black hair step through the ripple and into the room.

"What the…" Fox says.

Elsa's eyes glow yellow. She throws her hands to the side, the transformation to bestial paws already beginning.

"Whoa, whoa." I step between Elsa and Sarah. "Don't go ripping out throats just yet. She's with me."

Literally and metaphysically.

Chapter 9

Standing between a half-shifted werewolf and an all-powerful necromancer is not exactly how I'd intended on starting my vacation. Sarah stands in the corner of the room wearing an artfully torn Misfits t-shirt and some form of legging jeans that look terribly uncomfortable.

"How did she get here?" Elsa asks.

"That's a wonderful fucking question," Fox agrees.

"It would appear," I say, "she...travelled through the spirit world?"

Sarah gives me a smile. She's an eighty-year old woman shoved into a twenty-something body and it's creepy as hell. There's something off about her mannerisms. I hadn't noticed it back when I was terrified of her, or when she was repeatedly ordering my death. But now, getting a good look at her, something doesn't fit.

"I'm not the only one who's been messing with the veil," Sarah says.

"Yeah, about that," I say. "There are a couple of pissed off ghosts back at my place. Any chance you could tell me how to get them back through the door?"

"Ghosts don't listen to us. If you made the mistake of letting them through then they are here to stay."

"Well fuck."

It's fine, not like I planned on going back to the apartment anyway.

"Why are you here?" I ask.

Sarah takes a step toward Ethan. Elsa, still more wolf than woman, lets out a growl that reverberates in the back of my skull.

Sarah stops, eyes never leaving the wounded alpha. "I had come to ask Sam why he was still here. He told me he had plans to leave the city, but this," Sarah nods at Ethan, "this is a sight to see."

"He's not some side show," Elsa says. She's kept her head from turning wolf, but her blue eyes blaze bright enough to light up a room.

Sarah holds her hands up. "I'm not here for problems. Like I said, I came for Sam, but I might be able to help. This is sharp work, yes?"

"How do you know that?" Elsa's clawed fingers flex open and closed.

"I've seen it before." Sarah gives me a coy grin.

So, it's true, it was sharp magic that Lloyd used to kill my parents.

"I might, *might* be able to help him. Could I take a closer look?"

Elsa looks to me. "Do you trust her?"

"Honestly? No."

Sarah feigns a look of hurt.

"But she does know more about sharp runes than anyone currently in the room. And she kind of has half my soul."

"I don't even want to know what that means." Elsa transforms back. She's a six-foot tall, blonde woman built to make a Viking shield maiden look like a chump. Yes, Elsa is still plenty intimidating without the fur and claws. "Fine, but if anything happens to him, it'll be your life."

Sarah watches Elsa with an odd kind of amusement. It's clear she doesn't consider the werewolf a threat. No lie, there are far too many homicidal women in this room right now. I find myself inching toward the door, waiting for a spark to ignite the powder keg.

Elsa turns to Fox, who shrugs.

"Can't hurt, I guess," Fox says.

"Fine, but don't do anything without telling me first." Elsa steps to the side to allow Sarah a better view. The werewolf's shoulders are bunched up to her ears. She looks ready to snap back into the beast at a moment's notice.

Sarah crouches at Ethan's side. She slides her palm over his chest.

The magic in the air is stagnant, whatever Sarah's doing, she's not drawing energy to do it.

"This is complex work," Sarah says.

"Can you fix him?" Fox asks.

Sarah concentrates on a rune shaped like a spiral with an "x" in the middle. "Fix him? I'm not sure, but I think I can help."

"Help how?"

"Breaking a symbol," Sarah says. "The exact, correct symbol."

"Why not break them all?" Elsa steps closer to look down at the carvings.

Sarah shoots a glare in Elsa's direction. "This is complex work. The runes feed off each other. It's like trying to diffuse a bomb. The sharps used fail-safes."

"So, you can't completely fix him, but you can help him?" Elsa again.

"This one." Sarah points at the spiral. "I think if we break this one, it will release his slumber."

"You think?" Elsa says, incredulous.

Sarah shrugs and stands. "It's the best I can do for now."

"So how do we break the symbol?"

"Fox, you have a blade I assume."

Does Fox have a blade? What a question. Might as well have asked if the Mountain City PD is dirtier than all the brothels in the Glow.

With a flourish, Fox holds out a small blade.

Sarah holds up her hands. "I'm not going to be the one to do it. He's your alpha," Sarah says to Elsa. "If you want to save him, you break the spell. Take the blade and carve a line through the symbol."

Elsa looks at the knife like it might bite her. "What do you think, Orange Coat?" She asks Fox.

Sarah sighs and crosses the room to sit on Ethan's desk. Her gaze falls on the television, showing a commercial for hair repellent spray. The assholes act like the hairs are some stupid dogs you can spray with something bitter to keep them from chewing up their couch. I hope every asshole stupid enough to buy a can gets killed by a troll.

"I don't know," Fox says. She and Elsa both stare blankly at the blade.

Fuck. No guts, no glory. I snatch the blade out of Fox's hand and slash through the marking before any of the women can react.

To say Ethan wakes up with a scream, would be the understatement of the century. The sound is pained and primal and loud enough to shatter windows. I drop the knife to cover my ears, but don't get the chance before Elsa has me by the throat. She lifts me off the ground like I'm a damn child. My head bounces off a plaque from the International Firearm Association.

I grasp at some magic to defend myself and find Sarah pulling from the well also.

"Elsa, wait," Fox shouts.

Without releasing me, Elsa turns to look.

Ethan's eyes are open. He gasps for breath, but the scream has died down to some manly grunts. I'm a little jealous. I've died a couple hundred times and still shriek every time someone snaps my neck. Hopefully, Elsa doesn't snap my neck. It's a long ass drive back out here from my rebirth spot.

"Are you okay?" Elsa says.

"Wa...wa-dur." Ethan pants.

Fox rushes behind the desk and grabs a bottle of water. She unscrews the cap and holds the bottle up to Ethan's lips. Seriously? He's getting spoon fed and the guy who saved him is getting strung up by my throat?

"Eh-hem." I cough.

Elsa sets me on the ground and takes her place at Ethan's side. Sarah is still watching TV, but I feel her release the magic. She's playing it cool, but I bet she was prepared to throw down if things went bad. Our lives are connected, she can't let me die.

"Are you okay?" Fox asks.

"Better now." He grins. Bloodshot eyes, covered in a fever-sweat, and a tremor in his hands and the guy is still hitting on my wife.

I grit my teeth and swallow the jealousy. Fox is coming home with me, and this isn't the time for petty bullshit.

Elsa takes Ethan's hand. "What happened?"

"I don't know. I was out for a ride and then I woke up here. What the hell is wrong with me?" Ethan looks down at the cuts across his body.

"Bunch of sharps jumped you," I say. "Then we saved you. Then we saved you again."

Ethan smiles at Fox. "You came for me?" There's a glint of hope in his eyes.

"I came because I didn't want to see you dead," Fox says. "I care about you."

Ethan's chest swells.

"But I don't love you."

Oh, shit.

Ethan sinks about six feet into the couch. His whole demeanor changes and his expression looks as pained as his body.

I would almost feel bad, if he wasn't hitting on my wife.

"Well," Sarah hops off the desk and walks to Ethan's side, "now that that's over. I'm glad you're awake. We have business to discuss."

"Who are you, exactly?" Ethan stares at the ceiling.

"I'm the woman who is going to fix this city."

Ethan turns his head just far enough to get a good look at Sarah. He huffs a breath. "What is some kid going to do to save this city?"

"I'm going after Burgess. I want to unite the people of Mountain City, not just the standards, all the people of the city. This is big. I'm talking equal opportunity for *all* races."

"Those are some mighty fine words from someone who can't even vote yet."

Sarah ignores the slight, pushes forward. "Do you know who I am?"

"Should I?"

"I'm Burgess' wife."

Ethan raises an eyebrow. "I know the rich old standards like them young, but that's a little much."

"It's a long story, short version, this isn't my body. That doesn't matter. What matters is my husband built an empire on my parents' money and then cut me out of it. He married me for money, used me. The empire he has? It's mine and I aim to take it back."

Ethan watches her, while stealing glances at Fox.

"I am going after Burgess. My plan is to do it by uniting the people of the city and taking my place as ruler of the city by popular demand, but if that doesn't work I'll deal with him in other ways."

"Well, that," Ethan says, "sounds an awful lot like talk of killing your husband."

Sarah scoffs. "One way or the other, I'm going to bury him. I would rather do it with help from some friends." Sarah holds out a pale, thin hand. "Can we be friends?"

Ethan pushes himself up to sit on the couch. His body tilts to the side, unable to hold himself completely upright. That sharp work sure messed him up bad. The hair sniffs the air as he eyes Sarah up and down. The look is predatory, but not in the way of a creep ogling a pretty woman. It's the intensity of a predator measuring up prey. The alpha's gaze flicks toward Elsa. She gives a barely perceptible shrug.

Sorry, head of the pack means this decision is on you, mate.

Better him than me. Sarah and my souls are intertwined and I'm still not convinced I trust her.

With a grunt, Ethan reaches out. His giant mitt engulfs Sarah's petite hand.

"You seem genuine," Ethan says. "Normally, I'd be worried about throwing in with the wrong company, but with Lloyd's smear campaign raging full strength, how much worse can it get?"

The christening words of every shit-getting-monumentally-worse voyage.

Sarah smiles. "I'm glad we can be friends, Ethan. It will be a profitable decision for the both of us."

"Before we start talking profits and losses, what exactly is it you want from my pack?"

"First? A representative. I've got a press conference in…" Sarah takes out her phone and checks the time. "…exactly one hour, forty-five minutes."

So, Sarah either doesn't need hair support, or she was confident she could talk Ethan into an alliance. It's a bold strategy either way, and I'd bet her coming through the veil wasn't about me.

These fucking rich standards always thinking they're playing chess when I'd rather be playing solitaire.

"A press conference?" Ethan raises an eyebrow. "To what end?"

"To announce my plan to unite this city."

"And you need one of my people there why, exactly?"

"Well, a speech about uniting the people carries a little more weight when there are people united behind you."

"So, you need someone from the pack to say the pack is with you?"

"Yes."

"Will anyone else be there?"

"Not yet. I wanted to start with the strongest, and most repressed people in Mountain City. I will have lots of outreach with other communities starting today."

"And I'm guessing you want that representative to be me?"

He is the alpha, it would make the strongest statement. My gaze drifts toward the television again. As soon as we're done here, Fox and I are hitting the road for the beach. Who cares what happens in Mountain City?"

O'Malley is on split screen with some old gray fucker, clearly a mage. He's wearing a perfectly tailored suit, and has that look in his eyes like he thinks he knows all of everything. I get it, wizard's power is almost completely based on how much they know, so reading a whole lotta books is commonplace.

Mages come in two varieties. The ones who have never seen the real world because they've spent their whole life reading. These poor saps look like they'd faint at the first sign of trouble. Then there's the mages who have seen the outside of a book and they carry themselves like the baddest of asses. You can generally find them guarding the city's elite, like Burgess.

The caption bar on the TV screen reads: Cheap Sharp Mercs Ruining Bodyguard Industry.

"It would have been," Sarah says in the background.

I watch the silent mage make his plea for…whatever. Probably wants the sharps to stick with selling drugs.

"But in your current condition. I think someone else would be best."

This catches my ears, but I'm still focused on the TV. Not my clown car, not my jokers.

Ethan makes a growl from his throat.

Awww. She's offended his delicate sensibilities.

"Right now, you are…" Sarah pauses, for effect or trying to find the right words. Hard to tell which. "Indisposed. You are the pack alpha of the strongest pack in Mountain City. It would not be beneficial for either of us if you showed any form of weakness in front of the whole city."

The mage finishes bitching on TV. The screen widens to only show O'Malley's smug grin. A grin to say he's sure his pithy quips will show those shady ass sharps what's up.

"So who then? Elsa? She's my second in command."

That would make sense to me. Seems like a plan. Shake on it so we can get the hell out of here.

"Well…"

Sarah's tone catches my attention. It's the tone of a kid who conned their parents into asking what would make them feel better. Well…a candy bar would probably fix my tummy. Since you asked, and all.

"I was thinking maybe someone sympathetic to the hair cause, but not actually a hair could give a really good impression. It would show there are non-werewolves out there who care about your community and that you trust them to speak on your account."

The TV is no longer my biggest concern. I do not like where this conversation is going.

"And who, exactly, would I trust to speak on account of my pack?"

Sarah's gaze falls on Fox.

Fuck. I don't like this. When Sarah and I made our deal, she wanted Fox to rule the city by her side. Please say no, please say no.

"Fox would look great on television," Sarah says, "*and* she cares about you and your pack. In the past week she not only saved three hair youths from brutality at the hands of MCPD, she also saved you. A fact that we will not mention, I can assure you."

"I," Fox clears her throat. "I, um…"

Sarah *and* Ethan both stare at Fox with puppy dog faces.

My wife is a badass killer, and she will *not* be guilted into doing something stupid by the necromancer and the hair.

"She makes a good point," Ethan says. "You've been here. You know how we live, how we feel, how *I* feel."

Not a big fan of the emphasis on the "I" there, chief.

"And think of how great it would look," Sarah says. "This city has been run by Lloyd and his flunkies for too many years. Two women, powerful women, standing up to say it's been enough."

"I…"

"This could be big for us," Ethan says.

A part of me wonders if Ethan is suddenly all on board because he thinks it's a great idea or if he wants an excuse for Fox to stay around. I'm having a hard time discerning if it's the detective part of me or the raging jealousy monster part. Who says it can't be both?

Fox gives me a look. It's the pouty, blinky-lashed face of, 'please forgive me.' "Fine. One press conference until Ethan can get back on his feet."

Goddammit.

Ethan and Sarah give tiny fist pumps, both apparently deciding they are getting what they want out of the deal.

"Perfect," Sarah says. "You need to get cleaned up and changed. We have to be on the road in less than an hour."

Chapter 10

Fox is in Ethan's shower, cleaning up. I sit on the front porch smoking a cigarette. It's not even that I crave the nicotine, I need something to do with my hands. I wanted to smoke inside to be closer to Fox, but Elsa shooed me away. Apparently, werewolves have delicate noses or some shit.

Bitches.

On my third smoke, Elsa walks up carrying some kind of boss-lady-power-suit and a white silk camisole. There's a pair of flats in her other hand.

"Huh. I expected you to be more of a chain-mail or leather type," I say.

Elsa smiles at me. "Oh, I am. This came from Anna. She has a whole closet full of more clothes than she could ever wear." She leans in close. "Between us, she thinks she's Anastasia or something. Showed up here from Russia a few years back and acts like she's the toughest pup in town."

"So, you're a big fan of her then, yeah?"

Elsa shoots me a playful glare. "If she couldn't stand the cold, I'm not sure what she's doing here in the heat."

"So, I'm guessing she doesn't know she's contributing to Fox's wardrobe?"

"Oh, no, she knows. Ethan's orders. The look on her face was priceless."

I can't help but laugh.

"Do you want to take these up or…?"

"No, it's fine." I light up another cigarette. "I've gotta finish my cigarette."

Elsa shrugs and takes the clothes in the house.

My phone buzzes in my pocket. Again, with this bullshit? Who keeps calling me? I take out the phone. Blocked number. If this is about my car's warranty I'm going to scream. I slide my finger across the screen. "Hello?"

A heavy breathing from the other side.

Guess this isn't a sales call.

"Hello?"

A mad cackle. The voice sounds vaguely familiar, but I can't place it. I end the call. Fuck that.

Another two cigarettes and Fox comes down looking like she's about to run for mayor and kill the competition, literally.

"You look like a boss," I say.

"I never knew suffocation by blazer was a type of torture. I look like I'm about to interview a politician who got caught giving blowjobs in a gas station bathroom."

"Bet you'd nail his ass with hard hitting questions if you did."

"Awww, you're so sweet." Fox kisses my cheek, careful not to smear her light pink lipstick. She wraps her long red hair up in a bun at the back of her head. "Let's find Sarah and get out of here."

Sarah is easy enough to find. She's sitting in the back seat of a luxury SUV identical to the one I stole. The door is open and she's got one foot bouncing in the air.

"Nervous?" I ask as we approach.

Sarah closes a notebook and sets it behind her. "No. Are you ready?"

Fox shrugs. "What am I supposed to say?"

"Here." Sarah takes a page out of a binder and hands it to Fox.

"Is this some kind of script?"

"Not at all," Sarah says. "Scripts are strict, boring. This is just a general idea of the message we need to convey. Take a look at it but say whatever you feel when you get up on stage."

"You sure about that?"

"I trust you." Sarah pulls her feet inside and closes the door. "Follow us," she says through the open window.

Fox raises an eyebrow. "You hear that?" she says on our way to the Mustang. "She trusts me."

"Yeah," I say. "You're awesome. Only a dumbass wouldn't."

Fox giggles and kisses my cheek. "You really know how to make a girl feel nice."

My car's engine has long stopped hissing, but there's a suspect puddle of liquid under the engine.

I take the driver's side. "I'll drive this time. If it isn't dead."

Fox tosses me the keys. "If you aren't driving like you stole it, are you even really driving?"

What does that even mean?

I sit down in my seat and say a silent prayer to the pony gods. With one pet of the dash, I twist the key in the ignition. The engine roars to life, idles down low enough it seems like it's about to die, and then levels off at a steady thump. I rev the engine a couple times and the motor responds. Maybe not broken after all. I notch the car into gear and follow Sarah's SUV out of Hair Nation.

Fox spends the drive reading over Sarah's notes. From what I can see out of the corner of my eye, it's just a few bullet points, not a novel. As we get to the Downtown limits where Ethan was attacked, Fox says, "I know this isn't how you wanted to spend today. Trust me, I want to be gone more than you know. Especially, with Hisa in town."

"Hisa? Your mom?"

Fox nods.

"Why would you run from her?"

"I've been running from her since I left Japan. It's the reason I kept hopping bodies before I met you. Hisa hunted me from the moment I left."

This is news to me. I knew that Fox went on a string of body snatching before we met, leaving soulless husk after soulless husk in her wake. I did not know it was because she was running from her mother.

"So, since you spent however long running from your mom, is this really the best time to be going on TV with Sarah?"

Fox looks out the window. "She already knows I'm here. No point in hiding here anymore."

"Shit." What else am I supposed to say.

"It's fine. She has another daughter. She doesn't need me. She's just...stubborn." Fox crumples the paper and tosses it over her shoulder. The paper bounces off the bag of cash, falls to the floor.

"We'll get this stupid press thing taken care of, then I'll go make sure Ethan is healing up alright...if that's okay, and then we can get out of here." Fox bats her eyes at me and kisses the side of my neck.

"That's cheating," I say. "How the hell am I supposed to say no to that?"

"You're not." Fox pulls down the visor to check her lipstick.

The warmth from her lips burns on my neck. It's a feeling of love that radiates through my whole body. One favor for the idiot dog and then we can be gone.

The SUV parks behind the courthouse and I take the spot behind them. As I get out of the car, I can already hear a commotion on the street out front.

Sarah gets out of the car, accompanied by a mage with white hair and a tailored suit. The guy exudes hey-I-do-magic-shit vibes, and that's not including the bulge of a handgun tucked under his left arm.

A second figure steps out next to the mage. The figure is a fit person, ambiguous enough to be a man or woman. They are wearing black cargo pants and a loose-fitting long sleeve black shirt. Gloved hands hold onto a semi-automatic rifle. A balaclava covers their face with mesh drapes guarding their eyes.

"Is that a sharp bodyguard?" I ask Fox.

"Sure looks like it."

Sharps are bodyguards for people who can't afford mages. Sharps are durable, being already dead and all, and they work pretty cheap. The fact they are anti-magic often times makes them a good counter to mage guards as they cancel out the magic. A mage without access to magic is like a hair without a pack, a sad fucking sight.

Normally, sharp bodyguards are a shit show. Just some random vamp that got sucked into doing a job for enough cash to afford their next jolt of whatever. They are twitchy and jumpy and can usually barely manage to cover their skin with ratty clothing. This person, though, is a pro.

I've never seen a sharp with a gun that didn't look like it'd been used to knock off a half-dozen liquor stores. This one is ready to rumble. It makes me wonder if Sarah is expecting a brouhaha of the magical variety at this little carnival of hers.

This whole thing is starting to make me uneasy.

I creep over to Sarah's side. "A mage *and* a sharp? Is there something we need to be worried about?"

"Not at all, Samuel. Just making sure we have all the bases covered. Besides, this is about unity. What could be more united than a hair, mage, and sharp together showing their support?"

"It's beautiful really. I'm sure everyone will tell you so. Are you going to get a troll to hold up the podium for you?"

"Don't be crude." Sarah walks down an alley toward the front of the courthouse. She gives Fox a wave to follow along. "The trolls are digging their feet in the dirt, but I'm hoping they can be persuaded."

The trolls have been on standard payroll for as long as I can remember, and that's a long time. They act as the city's loan sharks, but really the silent backers are the humans. They give the trolls a job so they can feel special and smash on the poor suckers stuck taking payday loans in the Glow. If they ever start smashing the expensive furniture Downtown, it could be a real problem for the standards.

I lean into Fox's ear. "I'm going to circle around into the crowd so I can keep an eye on you."

"My hero."

"Hopefully not." I squeeze her hand and jog ahead. I circle around the podium and into the crowd.

A crowd stands gathered behind some police barricades. Reporters are up front, notepads at the ready. Behind them is a random mix of hairs, mages, trolls, and some stuff I don't recognize.

My phone buzzes in my pocket. I ignore it as I scan the crowd for potential threats. Magic swirls around the large crowd, impossible to tell if it's a lot of people taking little sips or one person swallowing up a nuclear blast worth of energy.

I wonder if Sarah paid people to be here, to make it look like a real hoopla.

The better question is if Sarah was smart enough to stash money from her husband. Lloyd hired me to bring her back into the fold. Once he figures out she's going for his throat, he's going to freeze her out of everything.

When he had Bartholomew reincarnate her dying body, it put her in a younger form. For as long as I can remember, Lloyd has been calling Sarah his daughter. I'm betting his daughter's name isn't on many checking accounts.

Then again, Sarah said Lloyd got rich off her parent's money. And she's gotten this far.

Camera shutters snap to life like machine gun fire. Sarah takes the podium in front of dozens of news station microphones.

She clears her throat. "Hello, citizens of Mountain City."

Chapter 11

Sarah smiles, letting her opening statement sink in for the crowd. Fox and the two bodyguards stand behind her. The tip of the sharp's rifle peeks over their shoulder. I can feel them scanning the crowd, looking for threats. The mage is doing much the same, old, green eyes ever watchful. Fox's hands clasp in front of her. She lets go, pushes her palms down her thighs. In a room of zombies, she's cool as a cucumber. Standing on stage she looks like she wants to bolt.

"I stand here today, in front of this wonderful city of ours, to announce change is coming to Mountain City." Sarah's voice carries across the crowd, proud, powerful. "A lot of you know already, but I'm going to say it anyway. Lloyd Burgess is my father."

The fact that she can call the old man her father without even a twitch means she's cut out to either run this city or ruin it.

A murmur passes through the crowd. I don't bother trying to suss out any of the words. They don't matter.

"My father has run this city under an iron fist for too long. He's promoted inequality among not just the races of Mountain City, but the income brackets as well."

This gets a small rise from the crowd.

"He's put all the city's money into the hands of one race, but control of all decisions are on his shoulders. He's appointed a puppet of a mayor and a hit squad of a police force."

A bigger cheer this time.

The mention of police gets me to checking the area again. Police barricades separate the crowd from the podium. Normally, I'd expect to see a line of cops guarding the front line, but there's no blue in sight. Apparently, the cops aren't in any hurry to change the status quo.

"I'm here today to announce things are going to change. Everything in this city will change for the better. I want to unite the citizens of Mountain City."

This gathers a large rumble of applause through the crowd.

"No more hairs can only do this, trolls are only good for that. For far too long, the races of this city have been defined as only one thing. No more. For no one is truly one aspect. Everyone should feel free to follow their dreams, and those dreams are what will make our city the best it's ever been. The best in the world, even."

This gets thunderous applause from the crowd. Seriously, how many of these people did she pay to be here. It has to be a non-zero amount. Has to.

Sarah smiles and waves and waits for the adoration to trickle off.

"With me today, I have three representatives from some of the great races of our city. Magnus Gustafsson, one of the leading mages of the city." Sarah holds her arm out to the man on her right.

"Lily Singh. She is one of the oldest sharps living in Mountain City." Sarah sweeps a hand toward the sharp on her left.

I know of Lily. She's not near as old as Darius, but she made a name for herself as a warrior who survived through ferocity. Darius is an aristocrat and survived through cunning and bribes.

Fox glances at the shrouded figure. A sharp bodyguard is one thing, but Lily is a big deal in the vampire community. Less than twenty-four hours after a pack of sharps attacked Ethan. And Sarah told us the hairs would be the only ones represented at this little shindig. My teeth grind, but Fox recovers quickly.

"Finally, Fox Flint, a close associate of Ethan Grisom, alpha of the Hair Nation, would like to say a few words." Sarah gives a small clap as she steps away from the podium.

The crowd follows suit and cheers for my wife.

Next to me, a standard guy in a business suit with a pink tie nudges a stone bro next to him.

"The hairs went and got a fine ass face," pink tie says.

Easy, Sam. Let them talk. It's fine.

Bro Stone laughs. The stones are gargoyles, but the trick is, they never know when they're going to turn to stone or for how long. Every one of them I've ever met is on some live-like-you-were-dying kick.

"Yeah," bro says. "I'd like to closely associate my rock between those thighs."

They laugh and fist bump like they've hit on a game winning pick up line. They straighten and eye Fox with a predatory glare. The men think they are wolves, admiring something they own.

My cheeks burn. A week ago, I'd have knocked their blocks off, but not today. I am new and improved Sam Flint. The energy of the crowd swirls in the air. Musky body spray lingers in the air, thick enough to taste. I take it in. It's not enough magic to draw attention, just enough, I hope to teach these fuckers a lesson.

While rolling the energy around in my body, I think on an episode of *Sex Sent Me to Surgery* I saw on TV once. I'd never known a urethra could be broken, and up until this moment I'd wished I didn't know.

The ruckus of the crowd silences individual voices, a homogenous sound that is less than the sum of its parts. I use that same energy to focus on drowning out the individual. Pink Tie and Bro Stone's laughs turn silent. A little bit of mute should help keep me from ruining Sarah's party or getting arrested by some dickhead cop looking to bust up the rally.

Tie and Bro share a confused look as I snap my finger. In a monumentally unfortunate turn of events, for the stone at least, the frat boy shifts into a gargoyle the moment before my world-ending snap. The guy is permanently frozen into solid rock. Stone breaks in time with the snap. Powder falls from the leg of his shorts, piling on top of his slip-on boat shoes.

Pink Tie screams. Well, he tries to scream but no sound comes out. Both his hands press against his crotch as he doubles over. He frantically looks around, silently screaming for help. A couple of trolls standing nearby cock their heads to the side without offering any aid. A standard woman curls her lip and moves further into the crowd. Pink Tie gives up trying to ask for help, and hobbles away from the crowd. Once he gets far enough, my silence spell will break, but Fox and I will be long gone before anyone has time to figure out what happened.

Fox clears her throat in front of the microphones. She stands tall, proud. I catch a slight tremor in the fingers of her left hand, a tell that I've noticed the two times I've seen her anxious in our marriage. She grips the podium with both hands.

"Hello, my name if Fox Flint. Ethan, alpha of the Hair Nation pack, asked me to speak on his behalf." Fox pauses, clears her throat. "We've heard Sarah's offer and the hairs are on board. They are a kind people; I've seen this firsthand. They protect the ones they care about fiercely and that doesn't only mean pack members. It could be you, too, if you let it."

Fox pauses. The crowd gives a cautious applause. She gives a weak smile and continues.

The energy from the crowd is still in the air. I start sipping on it again.

"For far too long you have been lied to. We've all been lied to about the hairs and their intentions. Ethan and his pack are good people. And I fucking mean people. Not hairs. Not werewolves. They are some of the best goddamn *people* I have ever met in my life."

I wonder if the six o'clock news has an expletive beeper on standby.

"Sarah is ready to give the pack the respect it deserves, and the pack is ready to contribute to the community in a real way. There is strength, real strength in our numbers."

Fox pauses to a slightly larger swell of approval.

"And if nothing else, it's time we showed the rich assholes in the tower who's really running this city."

I let loose the power I'd been holding, using it to pitch my voice in a few different parts of the crowd.

"Ye-aaahhhhhhh!"

The crowd digs it. Cheers erupt as Fox, Sarah, and the guards step down from the stage.

Alexander Nader

Chapter 12

As I push my way through the crowd my phone buzzes again. Fucking prank caller bullshit. I dig the phone out of my pocket and the screen reads: Burgess.

Well, this day can't get any better. I answer the call.

"What?"

"First, you take my money and fail to bring my daughter to me—"

"Fuck off with that grift. I know she's your wife."

A pause. Then, "Regardless of her relation, I hired you to bring her to me. Not only did you fail to do so, I see now you are in cahoots with the mad girl."

"Yup, that's me," I say as I push past a couple stones chugging beers while tightrope walking the police barricades. "In cahoots with the mad woman. Save your energy. I'm leaving town. You'll never see me again."

A ruthless laugh switches gears into a hacking cough. "Do you think it's that easy? That you can take my money, side with the whore, and then drive off into the sunset?"

"You married a woman you didn't like for her daddy's money and she's the whore?" I'm tired of fucking around with this rich old piece of shit. If he's going to spin off on a tangent, then I might as well wind him up some more.

The comment stops the old man in his tracks for a moment. "You stole from me," he says, choosing to ignore my wicked good man-whore comeback. "I will track you to the ends of the earth and when I find you, Samuel, I'm going to make you watch me carve a pelt from your precious Fox."

The call ends.

Mother fucker.

Thinks he can call and threaten me over a news conference? Whatever. The rich old bastard is going to have enough on his hands to worry about with Sarah's little coup. Fox and I will slip out in the night and he can duke it out with his wife for custody of the city. Maybe, if he plays nice, she'll let him have holidays and weekends.

An image of my dead parents damn near knocks me over. Thank you, subconscious. Yes, I know the bastard had my parents killed. Sarah promised to take care of his ass. Something twitches in my stomach. Sarah is running a war against him, a very public skirmish. The last thing any war needs is a martyr.

First, he killed my parents. Now, he's threatening Fox. He has enough money to track us down, assuming he wins his culture war. How often do coups fail? More often than not, if history is any indicator.

Do I really want to take the chance that Lloyd crushes Sarah and then comes after my ass? The old man can hold a hell of a grudge, that much is certain.

Shit.

I'm going to have to kill the old bastard.

Probably.

Now's not the time. I'll run it by Fox and see what she thinks. Given the thing with her mom, there's a chance we are going to end up on a parenticidal spree.

Once I get past the podium area, it's a clear shot down the alley to where we parked.

Fox and Sarah are standing by the SUV. I can see them arguing before I can hear them. The two bodyguards are at the back of the car. Lily has her gun in front of her and I can feel a slight draw of magic toward Magnus, but both are holding their positions.

"...would only be a hair rep and then you show up with a sharp?" Fox is yelling. "After what they did to Ethan? You lied in the worst kind of way. And you wait to spring it on me until I was up there, in front of all those fucking people." Fox takes a step back and cusses under her breath.

I set a hand on Fox's shoulder. She shrugs out from under my grip.

"My apologies," Sarah says. "I thought if—"

"You thought if you told Ethan the fucking vamps were backing you too, he wouldn't help. So you lied. It's a brilliant goddamn strategy but fuck you all the more for doing it."

Sarah smiles as she opens the door to her ride. "I meant what I said before, you know. Back at Sam's little cabin in the woods. We could run this city, you and me. Who would dare to stand against us?"

Fox paces a few steps in each direction. She stops at me, her face red with fury. "Do you have a smoke?"

I pass her a lit cigarette. She takes a drag deep enough to drown a giraffe before blowing a stream of smoke.

She shoots a glare in Sarah's direction before stomping over to my car.

"Nope," I say as she reaches for the driver's door. "You're pissed and my poor old car can't handle that right now. I'll drive."

Fox eyes me with straight murder before opening the passenger door. She slams it closed hard enough the window glass falls down a few inches. At least it didn't shatter.

"I'll be in touch," Sarah says.

Magnus pushes her door closed and slides into the driver's seat. Lily loads in up front and the SUV speeds off into the afternoon. Surely, bound for some penthouse where Sarah can sit upon her throne of eight thousand thread count sheets. Strategic plays of how best to manipulate her way to victory will play in her head like a game of 4D chess. She'll drink wine older than me and probably be fanned by a man-servant named Hans. Fucking rich people.

I sit in the car. "You good?"

"No. I'm not. Fuck that bitch. She lied to us."

"Not the first time."

"She fucking conned us."

"Also, not the first time."

There was that whole bit where she had me repeatedly killed so I could find my spine, or whatever the hell she wanted from me.

"She's a politician," I say. "A lifelong rich kid that's been through some stuff, but she's watched Burgess work for all these years. You don't run a city by not being full of shit."

"Are you on her side?"

"No. Fuck." I light myself a cigarette, just to do something.

Fox flicks hers out the window. I pass her mine, light another.

"I am used to being a pawn on their board. Lloyd used me for jobs over and over and I might have to kill him now."

"Wait." Fox turns to look me in the face. "What?"

I sigh. My head hurts. Images of the beach and my dead parents battle in my mind. "Burgess called me a second ago. He saw you on TV and he threatened you."

Fox's jaw sets.

"Yeah," I say. "I feel the same. Sarah said she'd take care of him."

"But she wants to dethrone him," Fox says. "That's far too slow. After what he put your family through. I get why you'd want to act sooner."

My phone buzzes in my pocket. Fox's chirps at the same time.

Please leave us alone.

Fox checks her screen, answers the call.

My phone says blocked. I answer anyway.

"If this is more creep show breathing, take me off your call list."

"Don't trust the necro," a raspy voice says.

The voice tugs at the edge of my memory, but I can't place it.

"Why?" I ask.

The call ends.

I squeeze the phone, trying to make it pay for everything it's done to me. The phone pleads for mercy, and I let up as Fox ends her call.

"You good?" Fox's turn to ask.

"Some damn crank caller. You?"

"Ethan wants me to come back. Said he wants to thank us for speaking for the hairs today."

I am sure that Ethan wants to thank Fox and not 'us,' but I appreciate her editing the statement for my benefit.

Fox leans over, her hand wraps around my neck, nails digging into my nape as she pulls me close. She kisses me with a passion that burns hotter than fire. The kiss is more than desire, it's a soul deep need. She's telling me something with her body, and I'm listening with every fiber of my being.

"You're always first," she says, sitting back in her seat. "Always."

I take her hand and kiss the simple diamond wedding band on her finger. Part of me wants to bitch about going to see the hairs and not just leaving the city. The bigger part of me knows I can't leave while Lloyd Burgess is alive.

Chapter 13

Fox and I need to calm down. As we drive up to Hair Nation, we roll down our windows. The late spring air is hot, but at sixty miles an hour it feels nice. Fox plays with the radio, finds a pop station. A boy with a soft voice sings about wanting to seduce a girl, or another boy, or both maybe. He seems undecided about it all. But the beat is nice and so is the weather so who am I to complain?

We are well out of downtown, the sun setting to my left, when I catch the pair of headlights in my mirror. The ultra-bright lights of a new, luxury vehicle flash in my rearview. A large SUV is behind us, maybe two car-lengths back. It's probably nothing, but the blacked-out luxury ride doesn't seem like hair style.

"What is it?" Fox's gaze dips to the side mirror.

"I'm not sure yet. Could be nothing." I ease on to the accelerator without downshifting. It's not a getaway maneuver, just curious to see if they keep up.

The speed limit on the winding road to Hair Nation is forty-five. I'd been cruising at a steady fifty but slide the mustang up to a healthy sixty-five. The pony's tires protest, but the car grips the road without too much effort on my part. The speed isn't break-neck, but if the SUV wants to keep up, they'll have to push the large vehicle.

I round an S-curve, keeping my speed steady. Pulling onto a quarter mile stretch of smooth road, I catch a glimpse of the headlights again. They close the gap on the straight.

"Definitely being followed," Fox says. Without turning her upper body, she reaches into the back seat and grabs her katana. "Where do we want to deal with this?"

My brain rolls with scenarios. I try to imagine a world where someone isn't about to jump us and come up empty. Whatever is up, they want something. Could Lloyd be on to us this fast? It's possible. Anything is possible when you have more money than enemies.

"Let's wait till we get to the warehouse," I say.

Fox arches an eyebrow, a silent question.

"I know it's not cool to dump trouble in their laps, but if it is bad, it would be nice to have backup. And if we are in some shit, it's likely because of Ethan making deals with the devil."

"You're one to talk about making deals with Sarah Roswell." Fox smirks, playing off the joke, but the words sting anyway.

How is it my fault? She was going to keep killing me until I did something. And the fact that she had no problem killing me on repeat didn't leave me a ton of options. All I wanted was to be gone from this damn city, but she's too hungry to let go.

I downshift to keep my speed as the road pitches up a steep hill. The SUV headlights are maybe three lengths back now.

"Care to hand me some fire power?"

Fox digs in the back again and produces the magic bazooka of a pistol. Four bullets left. Make them count. I set the gun in my lap, silently promising not to use a round unless absolutely necessary.

"I'm going to give the pack a heads up." Fox takes out her cell phone and taps on the screen. "I sent Elsa a text and let her know there might be trouble."

Two more curves and Fox's phone chimes.

"She said they're ready for anything."

"Good." Because I have no idea what's following us.

It's a tense few minutes up to the Hair Nation compound. I slide to a stop in front of the warehouse and jump out of the car. I tuck the gun into the back of my pants. The weapon speaks to me, calls a siren song of violence and destruction. The thing is a living, thinking entity. Not only that, it's hungry for destruction, an insatiable canon desperate to rip everything in range from this world. I ignore the cold steel and draw on some magic.

A handful of cars dot the lot, but no immediate sign of life. Fox warned the hairs, they are ready. While closing my door I scan the warehouse. A person is pressed down on the roof, high-powered rifle barrel extending into the night. Guess the werewolves are ready.

I reach into the night, trying to grab onto whatever magic is available. The magic tastes like tension. The werewolves might be hiding, but the magic doesn't lie. They are ready to pounce. There's probably a half dozen four-legged monsters prowling the tree line.

The anxious feel is cool and all, but I'm not sure how to use it, what kind of spell I can brew with sweat and nerves. I reach out further.

The magic, past the tension, just dies. It's weird. There's …nothing there. It's dead.

A roaring engine breaks my concentration. Burning headlights cut into my eyes like I stared into the sun. The SUV stops five feet from me. All four doors open at once. I try to focus the weird, awkward energy of a dozen keyed up werewolves into a useable bit of magic. Wonder if a ball of dog breath is enough to take someone out.

A foot crunches on gravel. Metal sings to life as Fox slides her blade free of the scabbard. Four mages step out of the SUV.

A scream from my left draws my, and the mage's, attention.

"The fuck?" I say. Turning to keep the mages in my vision while looking at the woods. The headlights are too damn bright. I can't see into the trees.

The scream of a man turns into a pained howl.

The mages seem equally as confused, but the distraction only lasts a moment before all four turn their focus to me. I can feel them grasping at the magic in the air, but I was here first. There's nothing for them to take. A flash of concern passes across their faces before each lifts a rifle in my direction.

I glance back and Fox is gone, vanished into shadows. Good.

A sound like a canon explodes over my left shoulder. A basketball sized hole appears in the driver door of the SUV as the driver drops to the ground.

Muzzle flashes light up the night.

Rapid gunfire drowns out the commotion in the woods.

I focus the twitchy hair energy into an image of a large wolf. A blue, phantasmal apparition appears in front of me. Bullets send plumes of blue smoke. The beast soaks up the lead like nothing.

The mages pause to reload. I command the spectral wolf forward. The animal charges, a silent flicker of a killing machine. Heavy footfalls shake the earth beneath my feet as a real, giant wolf sprints from the darkness.

The mage on the driver's side slams a magazine into place and swings his gun toward the wolf, but he's too slow. The animal bats the gun away and takes the man's head in its gaping maw. There's a wet crunch as the wolf tears the head off like a chew toy.

My ghostly wolf slams its paws against the passenger door. The supernatural strength pins the man in the frame. I feel him frantically grasping for magic, energy that I have a monopoly on and he isn't strong enough to take from me. The animal steps back and rams its shoulder into the door.

The man's panicked pull for energy dies as his lifeless body falls to the ground.

The mage in the back reloads and pops a couple excited shots in my direction. They miss wide. He's seen his three buddies die and is in panic mode. Mages are far too squishy for an up-close fight. The mage steps out to the side, I get a clear view of her now. Her white hair is in a neat bun on top of her head.

She squeezes off three more shots. She's not trying to hit me, just trying to buy time as she scrambles toward the driver's side of the SUV. I stand and watch like I'm bullet proof.

As she crosses the front of the vehicle, her back arches for a moment as she falls to her knees. Fox appears out of nowhere. Her metallic orange blade flashes across the night as she swipes down at the woman's neck. The mage's body falls against the front bumper as the head slides to the gravel.

Fox flicks the blood off her blade and puts it back in its sheath. She pushes a lock of hair behind her ear.

Howls and screams erupt from the woods to my left.

What the hell? All the mages are dead.

Branches snap. A canine yelp.

A familiar voice screams out for help.

Alexander Nader

Chapter 14

Fox and I sprint to the woods. It's full dark and my eyes can't adjust fast enough from the high beams of the mage's SUV. I'm running into the woods blind, trying to follow the sound of breaking branches.

A thunderous crash over my right shoulder as a large wolf races past me, knocking small trees and branches away like flies. I'm pushing as fast as I can, but two more wolves blow by, charging into the night.

Something screeches. Another howl.

Gunshots echo through the hills. Muzzle flashes give brief glimpses into the distance.

Flash.

Human figures fighting the three wolves.

Flash.

A man on the back of a wolf, arm wrapped around the beast's neck.

Darkness.

The action is fifty feet ahead. Heavy thumps draw my attention right. The largest wolf I have ever seen, black fur with a white chest, paws its way through the forest. The beast winces with each step. It moves in a slow gait, but its legs are so long it keeps pace with my sprint.

I'd put money on it being Ethan.

We reach the action together. My eyes have gotten used to the dark, mostly. Human figures move through the night, attacking the wolves. A pained sound to my right. The person riding a wolf repeatedly stabs at the animal. The beast raises onto its back legs and drives the person into the trunk of a monstrous oak tree.

Someone charges in my direction. Silky smooth skin glides through the night. His chest is bare, legs covered in tattered black jeans.

Ethan crouches, ready to pounce. The attacker leaps impossibly high into the forest canopy. No standard jumps that high. It's either magic or sharp. After the incident the other night, my money is on sharp.

The sharp dives, boot down, toward Ethan. I watch as the wolf sees the danger, but it can't push away fast enough. He's in too much pain. There's no time to think. No way Ethan can get clear of the curb stomp coming his way.

There's some juice left from the fight with the mages. I use the last bit to propel myself into the air. Timing it just right, I clear the massive wolf and shoulder tackle the sharp in mid-air.

The force drives the sharp's back into a tree. There's an audible snap, but I don't know if it's a branch or a spine. My hands scramble for purchase, come up empty. Nothing to stop the ten-foot fall back to the earth. I flail my arms enough to get my feet underneath me, but then everything goes sideways.

A muzzle flash lights up the night. I don't hear the gun this time, but the familiar, searing pain of a gunshot wound hits me under my left armpit. My body instinctively curls from the wound. I lose track of the fall, land on my shoulder and neck.

Blackness.

Fuck. I do not have the time to deal with being reborn. Every time I die, my body stitches itself back from scratch. The procedure takes time and dumps my new body in my birthplace, miles away from the fight.

Normally, my conscience floats through space, taking me back home. Something is different. My soul remains.

Is this what forever death feels like?

One day, I simply won't be reborn. No one knows where or when that will happen. Is tonight the when?

Excruciating pain burns my mind. I haven't moved, still with my body. In a new twist, I can feel my body. Which means I feel my neck as it snaps back into place like a dislocated shoulder. The pain is unbearable.

I've had my neck snapped more times than I can count. Having it pop back into place is a first. Hot lead burns between my ribs as my body pushes the bullet out of my body. I blink a few times.

Am I…not…dead?

Was I dead?

Am I alive?

I'm Schrödinger's Immortal.

Does that count as a death? I hope not. A cat's only got so many lives, after all.

So many questions. No time to ask them now.

My eyes are ready for the dark now. I can see figures moving through the dark. The sharps, I'm assuming they're all sharps, outnumber the hairs three to one.

Sharps are faster and have more endurance than the werewolves. Something about no blood flow to carry the acid that makes muscles tired. The vampires fight like berserkers on crack. Knowing sharps, they probably are high on something.

A vampire charges at Ethan. The wolf manages a weak-ass pounce. The sharp dives forward, it manages to knock Ethan onto his back. Ethan growls and thrashes, but he's too weak, the vampire too strong.

Branches snap behind me, as a stampede of the rest of the pack charges into the clearing. A brown furred wolf crashes through the sharp attacking Ethan. The wolf bites the sharp's throat and whips its head side to side. The sharp goes limp. The wolf drops the body and heads further into the fray.

I scan the forest, looking for Fox. It's too dark. No sign of an orange blade or red hair anywhere. My heart pounds as I search for her. The wolves, now with the numbers advantage, chase the sharps toward Vampire Valley.

Ethan, still next to me, pushes to his feet. The wolf slowly pads toward the fight. Anxiety pours off of him.

Something crunches and draws my attention. A sharp levels a shotgun at Ethan. He's too far away. My magic tanks are empty from stitching my dead self back together. If Ethan dies, Fox is going to kick my ass. Dammit. The magical hand canon sings a three-point harmony from my back. An angelic chorus calling for blood and viscera.

I draw the weapon. Magic rolls off the thing in waves. There's no need to aim. I point the gun in the general direction of the vampire and pull the trigger.

The bullet blows a hole through two different trees between the sharp and I before exploding the vampire. That's not an exaggeration. The magic weapon blows everything apart from the waist up. A pair of legs stand, frozen in time for a moment, before crumpling to the ground.

The wolf hunkered down from the explosion. Ethan rises and looks from me to the steaming pile of sharp legs. The hair snarls and trots into the darkness.

"The fuck was that?" I ask the forest.

The hairs have all gone off chasing the sharps.

"He's embarrassed." Fox steps out of the darkness. Her skin is slick with sweat. The sleeve of her politician's blazer hangs by a thread. She comes to my side and takes the jacket off. There's blood splashed across her face, but she doesn't seem injured.

"Are you okay?" I stare at the blood.

Fox wipes her hand across her face, examines the mess. "Yeah. It's from Elsa. One of those fuckers got her pretty good. Are you good? I saw that fall from the tree. It looked…"

"Graceful?" I offer.

"I was going to go with deadly."

"Yeah. That too."

"How are you here?"

"If I had to guess, I'd say it has something to do with Sarah's magic. That's a guess, though. I honestly have no idea." I spare her the details of my body stitching itself back together.

"Uh-huh," Fox says. "We should probably look into that."

"Probably. First, we need to figure out what the hell happened. The pack seems to have the sharp situation under control. Let's get back to the mages and see if we can figure out who sent them."

Chapter 15

The parking lot in front of the hair warehouse is quiet. The whole pack must have answered the call for help, or at least most of it. I don't know much about their tactics, but I'd guess there are still a few capable fighters here, guarding the kids and the elders.

The SUV is just how we left it, four dead mages scattered around the thing.

"Think there's any chance we find it registered to Burgess?" I say.

Fox opens the front passenger door, careful to avoid the blood of the mage who got squished to death in the frame. "Or Roswell." She digs through the glove compartment.

I take the driver's side, start digging through the center console. "You think she could have had something to do with this?"

"Maybe." Fox opens a zippered pouch, frowns, and drops it on the floorboard. "These rich assholes fighting over the city. We're all just fucking pawns. I'm not going to pretend to know their game."

She's got a good point.

Being caught between Burgess and Sarah is not my idea of a good time. Lloyd has to die. I know that much. Fox will agree with me if I ever get a second of people not trying to kill me to tell her about it.

Sarah pulled a con on me to get us to go all wonder twins. It's not like she's above pulling the puppeteer. She seems like she wants to help the city, though.

"If Sarah is trying to unite the city or whatever, why send sharps and mages?" I find nothing in the center console.

The entire car is spotless aside from blood spatter from the dead mages.

Fox shrugs. She backs out of the car, leaves the door open. I meet her around front. The headless woman is still slumped against the bumper. Fox rifles through the mage's pockets, comes up empty. No wallet. No paystub from Burgess Mercs for Hire LLC.

"I told Ethan you were nothing but trouble." A red-haired man stands in the parking lot, double barrel shotgun propped up against his shoulder. "Ethan, Elsa, the whole lot. No one would listen. And then you go and bring the enemy to our gates." Jaxon spits into the gravel, kicks at the wet rocks with his boot.

"Listen," Fox says. "I know you want to think you're tough shit, but you're not. So quit walking around flopping your cock around for everyone to see. None of us are impressed, pup, keep it in your pants."

Jaxon flexes his jaw, red creeping into his freckled face. "Call me pup one more time, woman."

Before Jaxon can utter another word, Fox has closed the distance. Her sword drops to the gravel. She raises her foot and kicks out at the hand holding the butt of Jaxon's shotgun. His arm swings backward from the impact, drawing the gun barrel forward. Fox grabs the steel with her hand and sidesteps around behind him. The gun twists from the hair's grip as Fox drives her foot into the back of the man's knee. His leg buckles, dropping him to a knee with Fox holding the double barrel to the back of his neck.

Fox breaks open the shotgun and tosses the two shells onto the ground. She clacks the gun back into place and tosses me the weapon. Seriously, honey, you really want to do this right now?

I don't bother asking. Jaxon is quickly becoming more than an annoyance and if hairs respond to one thing, it's the assertion of dominance. Kid, prepare to have your assertion handed to you. I set the gun on the hood of the SUV and lean back against the grill. Too bad there's no popcorn.

"You want to get in on this?" I ask the dead mage at my feet. "Five'll get you ten says she murders him without breaking a sweat."

The mage doesn't take the bet. That's fair.

"If you want to do this," Fox says, "let's go—"

Jaxon spins, throwing a handful of dirt and rocks in Fox's face as he rises to stand. She shuffles backward, swiping at her face. That dirty mother fucker. I reach for the shotgun on the hood, but Fox waves me off. Shooting him would be so much easier.

Fox blinks her eyes clear and takes a boxer's stance, fists up, body nearly square to her opponent. Jaxon takes queue and mimics her position. The wolf circles, his large body eclipsing Fox every time he's between us. The pistol at my back sings again.

Three bullets left. Can't waste them on a piss-ant.

The hair closes the distance, throws a straight right hand. Fox steps to the side and kicks the guy in the nuts so hard I swear his feet come off the ground. In all my life, I'm not sure I've ever seen a person kicked so violently in the ball sack. Jaxon wretches and collapses to the ground coughing.

Fox drops her knee on his chest.

He coughs, sputters, "What the fuck was that?"

Fox grabs him by the side of the face, pushes his right cheek into the sharp gravel. Sune saunters down Fox's arm.

"Do you know what this is?" Fox says.

Jaxon watches with a wide eye as Sune snaps at his cheek from the back of Fox's hand. Kitsune are rare, but Fox used to hang around here. My bet is young red did some asking around after we showed up yesterday.

"I'll take that as a yes," Fox says. "Now I want you to understand that I do *not* fuck around and if you don't keep your little yapper shut, I will boot your soul out of this husk of a body faster than you can bark wolf. Do you understand me, pup?"

Sune takes one step closer. The tattoo's head reaches on to Jaxon's skin as Sune licks his cheek. The big man whimpers. Apparently, the threat of having your soul forcibly ejected from your body can house break even the worst mutts.

Fox gives Jaxon's face one last shove before she rises to her feet. The white silk tank top is covered in dirt and blood. I'm guessing Anna's not going to want that one back.

Leaning down to pick up the shells as she walks over, Fox casually grabs the shotgun off the hood. She reloads it and tosses the weapon back to Jaxon. The gun bounces off his chest and lands in his arms. The kid looks half dazed. Was that lick from Sune just a lick, or did Fox give his soul a little push?

Whether it was the ass-beating, or the threat, the fight is all gone from the kid. His shoulders are slumped forward and he won't look either of us in the eye.

"You're too kind," I say. "I'd have let some ghosts eat his ass."

Fox sets a hand on my chest. "Maybe, you shouldn't go messing with ghosts until you figure out how to send them back."

"That's fair."

Commotion from the woods draws my attention. A buck-naked Ethan leads two dozen naked men and women out of the woods. When you lose your clothes every time you transform, modesty kind of takes a back seat to function. Ethan's chest is still carved up bad, but it looks like some of the runes have started to heal over.

The hairs should be joyous they ran off the sharps, or at least pissed the vamps were in werewolf territory at all. Instead, they all look like someone kicked a puppy. Not even a werewolf puppy that could take your leg off, just a regular old dog.

Ethan walks with a slight limp. He looks from Jaxon to Fox and me. His head quirks to the side for a moment, but he doesn't ask.

"What's wrong?" Fox asks.

Ethan shakes his head and walks toward the warehouse without a word.

"Ethan?"

He keeps walking.

Elsa stops in front of Fox. Lacerations cover the left side of her body, but the blood has stopped flowing. Hair healing ability should have the wounds closed by morning.

"It's Jordon," Elsa says.

"What about him?"

"They…" Elsa swallows. "They took him."

Chapter 16

"What the hell do we do now?" I ask.

The pack of hairs have split up. They are all bowed heads and shuffling feet as they stumble toward their homes. Some have cuts and scrapes, but the injuries mostly seem to be emotional. Hair packs are as tight-knit as a group of people can get. Losing one of their own is a hard thing.

"Let's talk to Ethan. What did Elsa mean they took Jordon? Like they kidnapped him?" Fox asks.

I met Jordon a couple days ago. Elsa, Gabriel, and Jordon talked with me while Fox was getting an arsenal from Ethan. Jordon's probably in his early 20's, seemed like a good kid. Whatever the hell is going on with the sharps, it's not good.

Fox and I make our way up to Ethan's office.

Ethan's got a pair of gray sweatpants on and he's in the process of pulling a t-shirt over his head. "Come in," Ethan says without looking. "Both of you." The werewolf sits on his desk and stares at his bare feet.

"What did Elsa mean they took Jordon?"

Ethan sighs. "Jordon was in the woods on lookout. I'm not sure how the sharps snuck up on him, but he was attacked right as the mages began their offensive."

I think back on the howl right as the mages exited their ride.

"The sharps and mages must have been in on it together," Ethan says.

"I'm not so sure about that," I say. "When Jordon cried out, the mages looked shocked. They weren't expecting whatever went down in the woods. Tactical get ups like that, if it was a joint effort they would have been ready."

Ethan scratches at the back of his head.

"That might be worse," Fox says.

"Why would two different groups attack us?" Ethan says. "I thought Sarah's big pitch was community. I saw her sharp on television with you, Fox. Sharps have now attacked my pack two nights in a row."

"If it was different, the mages were probably after us. They followed us up the hill." I take out my phone and call Burgess. He doesn't answer. I leave a voicemail saying, "You missed," and hang up. "Nothing like kicking the hornet's nest to see what falls out."

"The mages stunk of Burgess," Ethan says. "I could smell it from across the lot."

My phone chimes. I answer without looking at the screen, expecting Burgess. A different voice hisses in my ear, "I'm coming for you, Flint." The line goes dead.

"What was that?" Ethan says, probably heard the call with those canine ears.

"Nothing." I put the phone back in my pocket. "So, what happened with Jordon? Are you sure he's not still out in the woods somewhere? Maybe he got beat up by the sharps and is on the ground?"

Ethan shakes his head. "We followed his and the sharps' scent. They must have had vehicles parked on a side road other end of the woods. Scent died at the road, tire tracks picked up where it left off."

"Why kidnap a hair? Why the kid?"

"Why do this to me?" Ethan lifts his shirt. In the light of the office the cuts are visible. A few of them have healed up, a couple more are scabbed over, and more than half are still red slits across his skin.

The office door opens. Elsa steps inside. She's changed into sneakers, athletic pants, and a black shirt. "Hey, sorry. I had to clean up." Elsa winces as she pushes the door closed.

"Are you hurt?" Ethan asks.

"I'm fine. What do you all know?"

"We think the mages were Burgess, after Orange Coat and Sam. The sharps are something different, but we don't know what."

"So, what's the plan?" Elsa asks.

"We march into Vampire Valley and find our boy." Ethan squeezes the edge of the desk.

"I'm not sure that's a great idea," Fox says. "If your pack shows up in the valley, it could spark a war."

Isn't that what Sarah's already doing? This isn't the time or the place for my opinion, so I sit on it.

"Not if we go during the day and blow all their fucking houses down," Ethan says.

Elsa sets a hand on her alpha's shoulder. "I know you want to save Jordon. I do too, but Fox is right. We have to be smart."

"It's late now," Fox says. "I'll go in the morning, ask around the valley. A kitsune asking questions will draw a lot less attention than a pack of hairs."

Vampires aren't big fans of the daytime, go figure. Fox saying "I" is cute, as if I'm going to let her prance into fang territory by herself.

"You would do that?" Ethan blinks at Fox like a puppy.

I wish he wouldn't do that.

"Yes," I say. "*We* will. Jordon seemed like a good kid."

"Didn't you plan on getting out of town?"

"Consider it payment for the guns," I say.

That and I've still got to take care of Burgess before we split.

"The pack owes you its gratitude." Ethan opens his mouth, pauses. He swallows, says, "And I owe you mine." The desk creaks under the alpha's grip. "I shouldn't have been in the field tonight and you protected me."

Because my wife would kill me if I let you die seems like the wrong response. So, I go with a neutral, "No problem."

"First sign of daylight, we'll head out to the valley," Fox says. "In the meantime, we need to get home and get some sleep."

"Definitely sleep. Maybe not at home though," I say.

Fox gives me a confused glance.

"There might be some ghosts hanging out there still. They didn't seem exactly friendly."

"Oh," Fox says. "Shit."

"Yeah, that."

"You're welcome to stay at my place." Ethan pushes himself to stand. "One day off my feet and I'm buried in little fires." He nods at his computer. "If I get any sleep tonight, it'll be on the couch."

"You need to get some rest, build your strength," Elsa says.

"Whatever the sharps did, it's either healing or it's not. I can't sit on my ass and watch y'all do the work. Besides, do you want to go over analytics of Fox's perception at the press conference? The publicist I hired has some very pleasant color coding for his graphs on demographics."

Elsa cringes. Fox cringes harder.

"You had someone analyze me at the press conference?" Fox's hand rises up to the notch at her throat. Her normally pale complexion shows a hint of green. She might puke.

Ethan laughs. "Don't worry, Orange. The early poll results said you did great."

"Oh. Okay. Well, that's good." Fox forces her hand down to her side. "Are you sure about us using your place?"

"Yeah. Y'all saved my ass. It's the least I can do."

Fox looks at me, silently asking if I'm good with the offer. I give a subtle nod. It's late, we've been running non-stop for what feels like a month now. I'll take any bed right now. Doubly so if it's free.

Chapter 17

Fox and I sit together in Ethan's enormous bed. My pile of clothes on the floor smell like sweat and death. Hopefully, there is a runt of the pack around here somewhere that can loan me clothes until I can buy more.

"That was a day," I say.

"Yeah."

"You want a smoke?"

Fox shakes her head. "I can wait."

"Right."

The hairs and their sensitive noses. I imagine Ethan is already going to have these sheets burned when we leave. It's fair. If I could smell as well as they do, I wouldn't want my bed to smell like some other dude.

Fox sets her hand on my thigh. "Thank you for taking this all so well. I know how much it meant to you to be on the road."

"It's fine. I can't leave with Burgess alive anyway."

Fox slides down in bed so her head rests on my chest, a gentle smile on her lips. "That's the smartest thing you've said this week." She twirls a finger around the hairs on my chest. "What made you come to this brilliant decision?"

"Sarah. She's too smart. Back at my cabin, she said she'd take care of Burgess. I assumed that meant she'd kill him and get it over with, but this power play for the city is different. If she makes a move on Burgess' life, it'll go sour. Nothing like a martyr to end an argument."

"You don't think she'll kill him? After he married her for her parents' money, after he used her?"

"I'm sure she would like to, but I don't think she will. Not on a fast enough timeline anyway."

"You don't mind making a martyr?" Fox sets her palm flat on my chest and closes her eyes.

"Makes no difference to me who runs this corrupt town."

Fox 'hmmms' and takes a deep breath. I watch the steady rise and fall of her back as she drifts off to sleep. Sune curls up into a ball on the back of Fox's shoulder.

When Fox's mom tried to attack me…fuck, was that this morning? It feels like a week ago. Her tattoo had too many tales. Six, I think. I quietly curl up to examine Sune. How do foxes get more tales? Is it an age thing? Power? Sune shows no signs of growing a second tail. The tattoo cracks an eye, sees me staring down at it like a creep. She gets up and walks down Fox's back, disappearing underneath the covers.

Sneaky ass tattoo.

###

Warm morning light wakes me from a deep, dreamless sleep. Fox has rolled to the other side of the bed, taking all the covers with her in the process. A shiver passes over my body, what does Ethan keep his thermostat on, fifty?

I slide out of bed and pick up my clothes from last night.

Nope.

No way in hell am I putting them back on. I creep over to Ethan's dresser. Whoever said it is better to ask for forgiveness than permission probably wasn't dealing with a werewolf, but any port in a storm, right?

I find a pair of athletic sweatpants with a drawstring in the waistband and a t-shirt with a gun brand logo on the front. Not my usual duds, but it'll do. I leave Fox in bed and sneak downstairs for a cigarette.

Elsa is waiting on the front porch. Her blonde hair is pulled into a tight braid, and she's changed into loose fitting slacks and blouse.

"Security detail?" I take a cigarette out of the pack, catch Elsa's lip curl, and put it back. Elsa has been nice to me, no need to be a dick and light one up in front of her.

"Waiting for you and Fox." Elsa nods up at the loft and I catch a glimpse of a gun hiding in the folds of her shirt. "You said you would leave for the valley at first light. Gabriel and I are coming with you."

I blow out a breath. "Really? I'm immortal and she's a badass. We don't need babysitters."

Elsa shrugs. "Ethan's call, not mine. He's not wrong for sending protection, though. The attack on Ethan, kidnapping Jordon. It's dangerous work. If Ethan sent you on a job and anything happened, he'd never forgive himself."

"You mean if anything happened to Fox. I don't think he'd mind anything happening to me."

Three different memories of Ethan snapping my neck play in my mind. Burgess tricked me into fucking Ethan over, royally. It ended in jail time for Ethan, and a scar on the reputation the hair has been trying so desperately to save. I can't be mad at him, but I also don't expect him to be at all worried for my wellbeing.

"I'll go wake Fox up and have her get ready. Say, do you think Anna has any more clothes she would care to loan out? Preferably with less shoulder padding?"

Elsa smiles. "I'll see what I can dig up."

Back upstairs, I find Fox sitting up in bed. There's still specks of blood across her face.

"Hairs are itching to get a move on," I say. "Elsa and Gabriel are coming on a ride along."

"Typical Ethan," Fox says.

"Yeah. Elsa is hunting a change of clothes for you. Why don't you grab a shower and I'll make us some coffee?"

Fox stands up out of bed and kisses me on the cheek. "My hero." She winks and skips to the shower.

Chapter 18

Cleaned and coffee'd up, Fox and I are ready to hit the cold, dead streets of Vampire valley. We meet up with Gabriel and Elsa on the front porch.

Gabriel is dressed in jeans and a plain white shirt. He has made no effort to conceal the .44 magnum on his hip.

"Are we going to have a chat with some sharp friendlies or rhinoceros hunting, chief?"

The hair grins. "Ready for anything."

"Just don't fire that thing at anything within a mile of me please."

The magical gun buzzes with energy at my back. I've had the thing less than seventy-two hours and used half of the supplied bullets. The gun can calm its tits. The thing needs tucked behind 'break in case of emergency' glass.

"Do you happen to have something a touch more precise?" I need some firepower other than the magic canon.

"For sure." Gabe nods at Fox. "Anything for you?"

Fox shakes her head. She holds her orange katana up. Blades are the only tool in her armory.

"I'll meet you at the car," Gabriel says.

"We're taking the mage's SUV," I say.

Gabe nods and jogs back toward the warehouse.

There's no way I'm riding all the way to Vampire Valley with two giants like Gabe and Elsa stuffed into the back seat of the Mustang.

I climb into the driver's seat. There's a fist-sized hole where the arm rest should be, and some blood spatter, but it's no big deal. Fox takes the front, passenger side, careful to get in without touching any bits of crushed mage from last night. Elsa takes the back passenger side.

The keys are still in the ignition. I twist the key and the engine fires to life. The thing is new enough that it must have cut the headlights to save the battery, or one of the hairs turned them off last night. The engine quietly idles as we wait for our fourth man.

Gabe jogs out minute later. He stops at my window. The button to roll the window down is completely missing. "Just get in," I shout through the glass.

He shrugs and climbs in behind me. Passing a gun over my shoulder he says, "Here. It's a Glock 22, smallest thing we had handy. Don't go and tell me it's too big. Deal with it."

I take the gun and Gabriel passes me an extra two clips. The Glock is heavy in my hand; it's definitely not my old snub nose. It'll do though. Anything is better than wasting more bullets from the magic weapon. There's no good place to put the gun while sitting in the driver's seat, so I pop the arm rest and set the gun and clips inside.

"Who's ready to go visit some of the creepiest fuckers this side of Mountain City?" I pull the car into gear and turn toward the road.

There aren't any roads leading directly from Hair Nation to Vampire Valley. The two have been tentative neighbors at the best of times. So, what should be a five-minute drive as the crow flies, is an hour long trek down from Hair Nation and over to Vampire Valley.

We ride in relative silence until I make the turn toward the valley. Fox's phone chirps with a call. She checks the screen and answers on speaker.

"Hello?"

"Hey, Fox," Sarah says. "I'm glad I caught you. Lloyd has challenged me to a debate on O'Malley's show. It would mean the world to me if you could be there to back me up."

Fox glances at me. I keep driving. It would be a good opportunity to get close to Lloyd, but I'm not big on us chumming up with Sarah.

"We're kind of in the middle of something right now," Fox says.

"Is everything alright? You sound tense."

"Sharps kidnapped a hair last night. We're on our way up to the valley right now to see if we can find out who or why."

A pause.

"It's still early," Sarah finally says. "The debate isn't until five this evening. Do what you have to and I'll try to help. I'll talk to Lily and see if she knows who might be behind this. Meet me at the news station when you finish, and I'll let you know what I've found out."

Fox's turn to pause. "Okay, I guess. Find out what you can, and I'd appreciate it."

"Fox?" Sarah says.

"Yeah?"

"I meant what I said back at Sam's house. You and I, we could rule this city. Think of the good we could do. I know it hurts you to see how the people of this city are treated. You could change it. Think on it. Don't answer, just think on it." Sarah ends the call.

Fox tosses her phone into the console.

"We gonna go?" I ask.

"We'll see how bad this goes."

That's a solid plan.

I roll up to a red light. Two motorcycles stop in the left lane, a third pulls up behind. One I'm guessing is a hair, one standard, and either a sharp or another standard with a leather fetish, they're bikers so it could go either way. The standard is easy to spot, they all walk around like they've got some shit to prove since they are so…well, standard. I'm surprised they're not all bikers now that I think about it. All three riders are wearing vests with a patch of a large tree and the letters SOA beneath.

"What the fuck is SOA?" I ask.

Shrugs all around.

"The guy with the pony-tail one of yours?" I nod to the rider I assumed was a hair.

Gabriel sniffs the air. "He's a hair, but not one of our pack."

The bikes rattle the windows, and in turn my brain.

I try to roll my window down to ask them about their cool kids club. The button is still missing. "Hey," I shout through the glass.

It's loud enough to get the sharp's attention. The person is dressed head to toe in leathers, including a collar, wide enough to cover all skin between their shirt and full-faced helmet. The sharp turns to me, their eyes invisible behind the black tinted visor.

"What the fuck is S-O-A?" I shout. "Stupid Ol' Asshole?"

The rider gives me a middle finger. They stomp their bike into gear and tear off up the road, running the still red light. The standard and the hair follow.

"Guess it doesn't stand for Safety Only Advocates," I say.

Fox twirls a switchblade around her fingers.

The light turns green, and I ease onto the throttle. We need to get in and out of Vampire Valley with as little fanfare as possible. Although a fight with douche-bag bikers sounds like a blast, our agenda is already full for the day.

A mile outside the valley, my phone buzzes. I ignore the call. The last thing I need is my new stalker to breathe in my ear some more.

As we cross the threshold into Vampire Valley, the energy in the air goes flat. The magic that's normally part of the atmosphere isn't allowed here. The sharps suffocate it. Even the gun at my back quiets to a whisper. The no frills gunpowder and lead of the Glock is looking real damn fine about now.

The first bit of housing in the valley is a series of townhouses, low rent places for low value sharps. It's the best place to start. I turn in to the first parking lot and kill the engine.

"Alright," I say. "Who's ready to go kick in some doors?"

Chapter 19

We exit the vehicle. I swap the magic gun for the Glock. The bullets are precious, and the magic doesn't work here anyway.

There's a group of kids to my left, and a group of adults to my right. The kids are all gathered around a sharp, sitting on a bench playing an accordion.

Fuck me. I hate this place already.

"You want the bard or the doors?" I ask Fox.

Open Doors are the saddest part of Vampire Valley. Sharps can't bite people without invitation. The doors charge vampires to feed. It's a lot 'safer' than it sounds, safe being a relative term in this case. If anyone rescinds their invitation the sharp has to immediately quit. It keeps the doors from ending up a pile of drained corpses. And hanging around on sidewalks all night is significantly less menacing when the entire valley population has dicks that don't work, lack of blood flow is a serious drawback of being dead.

"Accordion," Fox says. "I've never seen one played, maybe he'll be good."

"Elsa, Gabe, you think you can handle the doors over there?"

The wolves grin, wolfishly.

"Don't eat or kill anyone," I say. "Be discrete." I wish I still had my bag of cash to bribe something out of them, but it's probably for the best. That's my retirement fund.

The wolves drop the grins and head for the doors.

Fox and I make our way over to the kids.

The three-story townhouses loom over us. There are no windows in Vampire Valley, a safety feature. This close to the edge of town the sharps are packed in like sardines. I wouldn't be surprised if a few doors live here, too. It would beat the trek in and out of the valley every day. Ain't no public transportation coming out here, that's for sure.

The bard sits on the porch of the first apartment in the row. He's playing something that resembles a sea shanty. I can almost taste salt water in the air. The sharp wears a dark blue, full body morphsuit. The spandex covers top to bottom, but he's also got on a pair of tattered slacks and a button up shirt. The sleeves are rolled up to the elbows. A fedora sits on the back of his head, waiting for a stiff breeze to blow the stupid thing away.

The kids turn as we approach, all hungry faces and sunken cheeks. They could be anywhere between five and twenty. I suck at standard ages. The group eyes us warily. The smallest kid of the bunch, he's wearing overalls with no shirt underneath, sprints behind the apartments.

Great. I give it two minutes till someone gives us the 'fuck off' treatment.

The bard continues playing his tune but slows the pace as we approach.

"Hello," I say. "My name if Sam and this is my wife, Fox. We're looking for a friend of ours."

"If you here looking for yer friend," bard says, "I'm guessin' he's already dead."

The kids snicker.

Fuck everything that is holy. We should have picked the doors.

"Hey, I know you." A little boy with matted brown hair points at Fox.

She shakes her head. "I doubt it."

"No, really," the kid insists. "Where do I know you from?"

"Just one of those faces, maybe." Fox turns to the bard. "But really, it's important that we find our friend. He was taken last night."

"I doubt we made him go missin', as we do nothing without permission." The bard squeaks a happy little interlude.

Has anyone ever been beaten to death with an accordion?

I flex my hands, trying to keep my cool. "Our friend is a hair. A group of sharps attacked us last night and they took him away."

The sharp continues his tune, either done talking or doesn't have a witty rhyme.

"Please," Fox says, genuine concern in her voice. "Jordon means a lot to us. We just want to get him back."

"The answers you seek here are lacking, it's best now you get to packing."

"Fuck this rhyming idiot," Fox says. She turns to the kids, still watching us. "I'll give a hundred bucks to anyone who can tell me who would kidnap a hair and why."

The kids exchange nervous glances. The brown-haired kid is still staring at Fox.

"Wait a minute," he says. "I know you. You were on the tube. Talking with the pale girl about bringing the city together."

"Oh, shit." This from a girl with a dirty face and a Pokemon t-shirt that hangs to her knees. "He's right. It is you. They were playing it on the news all night."

The accordion player hesitates for a beat. His posture loosens. Even behind the mask I can see him examining Fox.

Fox glances at me, shifts her weight from one leg to the other.

"Fucking right," this is from a black kid with a spiked mohawk. The teenager has ripped black jeans tucked into a beat-to-hell pair of Doc Martens boots. "The sharps down this way, they was whispering about the two of yous all night. The fangs down this way, they like you."

Fox's cheeks burn red. She takes a breath. "So, you'll help us find our friend?"

The bard squeaks a little ditty. "The fangs on your side live on coal, kidnapping hairs, that could only come from the hole."

What the hell is with this guy? "What the hell is with that guy?" I point to the bard.

Mohawk grins at us. "The old one used to be in some Brit rocker band back in the day. Now, he sits up here and gives his rhymes away."

The other kids smile and clap.

Fucking hell.

"Whatever," I say. "So you think that kind of thing would have come from high up the chain then?"

"The sharps down here are only worried about their next meal and maybe a jolt of something to take the edge off." Mohawk hooks his thumbs into his pockets like he's got it all figured out. Kid isn't even old enough to drive.

"Nah," the kid continues. "No reason anyone on the edge would mess with the hairs. The mutts don't have anything to offer but guns."

Well, shit.

"Thanks," I say.

Fox eyes the kids like she might get something else out of them, but they are done. The lost punks have spilled their daily allotment of secrets.

"Let's get back to the car." I hook my arm around Fox's and lead her away.

"They showed up with their dicks in their hands, and an empty list of demands," the bard croons as we walk away.

"The fuck was with those kids?" Fox asks.

"Have you never been out this way?"

She shakes her head.

"They have a name, but I don't know it. It's German or Icelandic or some bullshit. I call them the lost punks. Just a bunch of orphans that run around. Their parents are dead or good as dead. They kind of banded together and no one ever stopped them."

"Why don't the sharps run them off?"

"No idea. I think the kids mostly hang out during the day and get scarce at night, not like the sharps can go biting them without permission."

"Weird." Fox rubs her hands on her arms.

"Not half as weird as those sad shits." I nod to the pack of open doors.

Elsa and Gabriel are walking away, both faces red with anger.

"Looks like that went about as well for them."

We load up into our ride. I start the car and ease out of the parking lot, aiming deeper into the valley.

"You all get anything?" Fox puts her feet up on the dash.

"Whole bunch of nothing," Elsa says.

"You'd think people who hung around vampires all day would be more in the know," Gabriel adds.

"We started at the bottom of the chain," I say. "We might as well be asking minnows what the sharks' dinner plans are."

"So why start with minnows?" Gabriel says.

"Because I'm a minnow and don't want to be swimming with sharks right this moment."

That sounds all smart and witty, but I'm also aiming our ride directly into deep waters. No one ever accused minnows of being intelligent, though.

Chapter 20

The deeper you get into Vampire Valley, the richer the sharp. After the condos and townhouses of the lowlifes, we roll into a section of dilapidated mansions from the turn of the 20th century. The houses would all be beautiful if they had windows. Instead, they look like pretty little prisons.

Houses in the valley house multiple 'generations'. Sharps can't procreate, but if a vampire turns a person they become like children. From my understanding it's not all master and servant bullshit like the kinksters would have you believe. They really do just act like family units.

"What are we looking for, exactly?" Elsa eyes a large pink house with black shutters.

"Someone to talk to. Unless you want to start knocking on doors in sharp town at noon."

Elsa crosses her arms and sits back. Who knew hairs were so impatient?

I spot what I'm looking for and click on the blinker.

"Seriously, Sam," Elsa says. "A mall?"

The shopping mall, a giant building with no windows and shit to do for the day-owl sharps. It will be quiet during the day, but that's fine. The people I'm looking for are always near. I circle the parking lot once, twice, three times before I spot what I'm looking for.

An old police Crown Vic sits parked with the trunk open. A skinny white guy rests on the bumper, playing on his phone.

"Fox, how much money have you got?"

"Couple hundred."

"Alright. Let me have it. Everyone, stay here," I tell group.

Drug dealers get suspicious about crowds.

I get out of the car and start toward the dealer. He sees me coming and slides his phone into his jeans, tucks his hand into his jacket pocket. The snub nose poking at the fabric makes me jealous. Wonder if he wants to trade for the Glock. I approach slow, feeling out at the air for magic. There is none.

"Hello, friend," I say.

Friend gives me a faint 'sup of a nod. He's got three fang tattoos under his eye. Supposed to mean he's killed three sharps, but I don't see it. His eyes are red and watery from smoking, but there's no killer behind them. It's all posturing.

"What're you in the market for?" He's still leaned against his bumper, finger on the trigger. The guy might not be a killer, but he's not an idiot either.

"A little bit of information is all."

He laughs. "Shit, bro. Information? You might as well try to buy a vial of o-neg spiked with heroin. It'd be cheaper."

Sharps are dead. Dead means no blood flow. To get high they go through a whole fucking process. One part blood, one part drug of choice, one part epinephrine, and one part stolen defibrillator equals a high lasting anywhere between thirty seconds and an hour, depending on drug and voltage.

I hadn't caught it at first, but the 'bro' gives him away. The dealer isn't a standard, he's a stone. Interesting. I've only ever seen stones at frat parties shouting about some bullshit.

"You're a stone," I say.

"And you're wasting my time," he snaps back. "What're you buying?"

I take out the cash from Fox. "A little information if I could? Jimmy sent me your way."

Jimmy is, was, a blood dealer from down in the Glow. It's a little bit of a gamble, assuming one blood dealer knows another. It's a huge gamble to assume the guy doesn't know that Jimmy got killed by a zombie in a hotel room four days ago.

The dealer narrows his eyes and sizes me up all over again.

A couple in trench coats and plague doctor masks walk by holding shopping bags from Belk. One of them looks in our direction, gives a beaked nod at the dealer.

The stone gives them a peace sign and tilts his head back. Seriously? A peace sign?

"So, Jimmy sent you, huh? How's that old sonuva bitch doing?"

"Oh, you know Jimmy." I smile and hope that means something.

The dealer busts out laughing. "Fuck yeah I do." He slaps his knee. "I'm surprised the dumb bastard isn't dead yet. Slinging crimson down in the Glow like some kind of animal."

Hey, I live in the Glow.

Lived.

Whatever.

"Crazy, huh?" is the smartest response I can muster.

"Alright. If Jimmy sent you, you're good people in my book." The dealer's hand slides out of his pocket and sets his hand on his trunk. "My name's Perry."

"I'm Sam."

"Nice to meet you, Sam. So, what kind of information are you looking for, bro?"

I step in close, pretend to be perusing the wares in Perry's trunk. There's a briefcase locked closed on one side, a few handgun carrying cases on the other. A large glass bong shaped like an octopus takes up the center of the trunk.

"A group of sharps snatched a young hair last night. I want to find out who."

Perry squints at me. "Man. Good joke. What would a bunch of sharps want a hair for? Sharps aren't exactly in the dognapping business."

"I would have thought the same thing, but I saw it with my own eyes." It's a small lie, but I'd like to keep as much distance between myself and the pack as possible.

Shady dude asking questions is bound to get quietly whispered throughout the valley tonight. Better than shady hair flunky.

"Have you heard anyone up to anything weird?" I pick up a carrying case for a Sig Sauer. The case is light, maybe empty.

Perry laughs. "Shit, bruh. This is the valley. Everything that happens here is weird."

I drop the case back into the trunk. "Have you heard anything about someone making a move on the hairs?"

"No. Hell, if that goth chick and red-head are to be believed, we're all coming together. All the people, man." Perry sniffs. "It'll be beautiful." He taps some white powder onto the back of his hand and snorts it.

This is why stones shouldn't deal drugs. That and having their stash raided every time they randomly turn into a rock.

"I gave you two hundred bucks, and this is all I get? You're worthless."

Perry holds a hand over his heart. "That really hurts, dude. You should go see Marvin the Muse, listen to some nice vibes and chill the fuck out." Perry laughs at a joke that's only funny to him.

"Give me my cash back."

"Fuck you. No refunds." Perry slaps his hand on a piece of paper taped to the underside of the trunk lid, 'No take backs'.

I take the Glock out from my back, slowly. Perry reaches for his snub nose anyway.

"Easy," I say. "Just want to sweeten the pot. What will this get me?"

Perry eyes the gun. I drop the magazine and rack the slide, emptying the chamber. He reaches for the gun and I slap his hand away.

"You already pocketed my cash. If you want the gun you've got to give me something real."

Another narrow-eyed stare from the stone.

I sigh. "Give me usable intel and you can have the gun and will likely never see me again. Or I toss your ass in this trunk and drive this dopey ass car off Moonshine Ridge without a second thought."

Perry makes a click through the edge of his teeth. He takes a glance around the lot. It's empty. "If you're for real, that'd come from deep in the valley."

I open my mouth for a 'no shit,' but he carries over me.

"I'm talking real deep. No mid-level sharp is going to fuck with the hairs without reason. Whoever you are looking for, they're old AF."

"Old AF? The fuck does that mean?"

"Exactly," Perry says.

I want to go home.

"So what? Darius? Chioke?" If I knew more old vampires off the top of my head, I'd name them too.

Perry shrugs. "Could be. Them and Lily are the top dogs. Dogs that between you and me, aren't getting along so hot."

It's a surprise, but not a shock. Sharps go through spats every couple hundred years. A five-hundred-year-old sharp gets tired of taking shit from a millennia old vampire and they duke it out leaving a trail of cold, black blood in the streets. Lily and Chioke are both old enough to want their shot at being top dog, but as long as I've been alive all of the coup d'fangs have ended with the old Persian on top.

"No one else doing some rogue shit?" I ask, trying to get every ounce of information I can.

"Probably, but if they are they're doing it quietly. We done now?" Perry holds out his hand.

"One more thing. If I wanted to hide a hair prisoner here in the valley where would I do it?"

"Have you seen the sizes of the old ones' mansions?"

Technically, I have not. That deep into Vampire Valley is not my idea of a good time. This doesn't seem like a good time to mention that, so I just nod.

"They could keep a whole damn army captive in Darius' estate and it wouldn't be a problem."

"Fair enough."

Perry eyes the gun in my hand. I check the side. The serial numbers have been filed off, as any good arms dealer would do before an unsanctioned trip into enemy territory. Seems harmless enough. I toss the gun to Perry and wish him a splendid fucking evening.

Chapter 21

I hop back in the SUV to an immediate, "Did you give my gun away?" from Gabriel.

"I thought it was my gun?"

Before word can spread through the valley that a bunch of weirdos are asking questions, I start up our ride and pull out of the parking lot.

Gabriel grunts.

"What did you find out?" Elsa asks.

As I lead us back toward the city, I tell the group the little bit I discovered.

"That's it?" Gabriel asks. His legs press into the back of my seat. "You got jack shit and now we're tucking tail?"

"It's not nothing," I say. "If Perry was being truthful, this isn't some rag-tag group of stray cats. If it really is one of those three, the four of us are going to do fuck all about it, day or night."

"What are we going to do?" Fox sits with her back pressed against the door, looking at me.

Why do I have to have a plan? The phone in my pocket buzzes. There's no point in even looking.

What would any of the sharps have to gain by pissing off the hairs? If it's really about a rebellion, why would anyone *choose* to fight a war on two fronts? Something isn't sitting right.

I scratch at the back of my head. Nope. No good ideas there.

"What time is it?"

Fox checks her phone. "Quarter to three."

"Shit. Are we going to Sarah's thing?"

Fox sighs. "I'd really like to find something, anything on Jordon."

"She said she might be able to talk to Lily about Jordon."

"If Lily isn't in on it," Elsa says.

"Even if she is," I say. "We can pick up something from her non-answers. It's up to you, Fox. I've got your back whatever."

Fox bites her lip. "She just said she wanted me there, not that I had to be on TV, right?"

"I think so."

"Fine. We can go, for information if nothing else."

"Okay. We both need clothes that fit. Elsa, Gabriel are you all good to split up? Head back up to the Nation and give Ethan an update?"

Gabriel grumbles something behind me. Is he really this pissy over a Glock?

"That's fine," Elsa says. "How are we going to split up with only the one vehicle?"

We roll to a stop sign at the outskirts of Vampire Valley. The tingles of magic tickle the back of my brain. Welcome back, new friend.

Across the street is a small diner shaped like an old camper trailer. Neon lights, too weak to cut through the afternoon sun, cover the giant tin hot dog. Three familiar motorcycles are leaned out front. Nothing like a little grand theft auto to make you feel alive.

I turn into the lot and park near the exit. The bikes are directly in front of windows, fully visible from the dining room. Too bad, the biker's seats are to the far left of the tin can and the exit door the far right.

"You up for a ride?" I wink at Fox.

She looks at the bikes, then grabs me by the face and kisses me on the lips. "I love you." She hopes out of the car and skips toward the bikes.

"You guys might want to split. There's going to be some real angry bikers here in about thirty seconds." I grab the magic handgun out of the center console and tuck it at my back as I exit the vehicle.

Gabriel opens his door and takes the driver's seat as I walk toward the bikes. He slams the door and speeds off out of the parking lot. Dude really needs some Ketamine or something. Shit.

As I walk, I swirl the magic around in my head. The magic tastes of kitchen grease and exhaust fumes. I could bathe in this kind of energy. It's a beautiful thing.

Fox throws her leg over a vintage Bonneville café bike. I'd planned to use magic, but she's already twisting wires in the ignition. She rises and kicks the bike to life. A throaty exhaust booms across the parking lot. That's my cue to move.

I jump on a Buell with an engine bigger than half the cars on the block. It's not my first choice in two-wheeled rides, but thieves can't be choosers. With a magical twist of the ignition the engine roars to life like an angry little monster. The bike settles into a lopey idle, a two-wheel muscle car.

Fox clicks the Bonnie into gear and tears out of the parking lot in a blur. I follow suit. Pulling out onto the road, I twist the throttle and really open up. The ground shakes beneath me.

We're still at the outskirts of downtown, so we get a couple miles of fun before things like traffic and stop lights ruin the good time. Fox has a head start. In the distance, I watch sparks fly from the peg as she leans into a sweeping right turn. I twist the throttle hard, playing catch up. The front end gets light as the bike picks up speed. I brake coming into the turn, but it's too fast. Leaning hard to the side, the bike feels like it's about to slide out from under me. My body tenses as I prepare for impact.

By some chance of luck, I make it through the turn in one piece. My burst on the straight caught me mostly up to Fox. I spend the rest of the ride flooring it on the straights and over-braking for the corners. The monster engine on the Buell is enough to keep up with Fox pushing hard on the vintage motorcycle. We coast to the stop light at 30th Street that signals the official entrance to the business district.

"Too slow," Fox yells over the sound of the idling furies. She blows me a kiss. Sune is crouched on Fox's neck, like she's bracing herself from the wind. The tattoo's fur looks ruffled from the ride.

Smart ass.

"Where to?"

We need clothes. Clothes require money. All our cash is in my car back up at Hair Nation and there's no time to go back. I check the bike's storage, come up empty. Guess the bikers are smart enough to keep their wallets in their pockets. We'll figure something out.

"Second Life," I yell.

Fox nods. The light changes to green. Fox takes off, splits lanes of oncoming traffic to pass a car. I do my best to keep up. The dense traffic of downtown, it's less a test of prowess and more a game of chess. Fox smiles ear to ear as she cuts off a BMW. The owner honks and shakes his fist out the window. As I ride by, I kick the mirror off his shiny new ride.

He shouts something but the engine drowns out the noise.

Second Life is a used clothing store at the edge of the Glow. A lot of the lower income folks from Downtown shop there so the place manages to keep a decent line of nice clothing. Where they get all the older suits and dresses and such from, I'll never know.

The thirty-minute drive from Downtown to the Glow takes eighteen. We should have really looked into two-wheel transportation years ago. I haven't ridden a motorcycle since an unfortunate incident on a pre-war Indian left me splattered across a Denny's billboard back when Elvis was still cool.

Second Life is in a small shopping complex between a nail salon and a sandwich shop. My stomach growls. When the fuck did I eat last?

I roll up next to Fox, leave the engine running. The cars parked near the doors are all boring sedans. Entry level executives trying to find some clothes to fit in with all the sharks. Don't do it, kids. The corporate world of downtown will eat your soul faster than an Ammit. Lucky those creepy fuckers never leave the desert. Nasty bastards, they are.

At the back of the lot, I spot a handful of people gathered around an old pickup truck. At least three have brown bags in their hands.

"Go ahead inside," I say to Fox.

She sets down the kickstand and heads for the door.

I ride over to the pickup and kill the engine.

The loiterers eye me suspiciously.

A stocky guy with chest hair and a beard that are inseparable sits on the tail gate. He swings his legs and watches me with a grin.

"What do you want?" He takes a puff off an e-cigarette.

"Wanted to see if anyone is interested in a rental."

The guy eyes the ignition, a half-smirk behind a wall of hair. "It's a sexy bike. How long's the rental?"

"Probably good for a few days if she stays in the Glow."

"Yeah." He pets his long beard, pulling the bottom into a point. He checks his crew.

A tall guy with greasy hair and a girl that's all twitches and shakes stare at the ride with hungry eyes.

"How much?" Beard says.

This is the best part about the Glow. You can find reasonable people who know what's up. There is no con, they don't bury their shit. The shit is on display for everyone to see. If you can't stand the smell, have fun in your glass tower litter boxes. Me? These are my people. Desperate, hungry, and dying for a good time.

I shrug. "Five hundred."

Sam Flint bargaining one-oh-one, aim high then take whatever they'll give you.

Beard laughs. His crew joins in. The twitchy girl watches the party to see when she's supposed to stop laughing, goes too long anyway.

"This truck didn't cost that, and I have a title for it." Beard bounces. The shocks squeak.

"It's a joy ride, not a long-term investment."

The magic in the air here is thick. I take a sip and snap my finger. The Buell thunders to life. I twist the throttle a couple times. The exhaust roars throughout the parking lot.

Something moves behind slick's eyes. The hungry look that druggies get right before they rob their mom. He's sizing me up. If Beard can't cut a deal, he's going to take the bike anyway. Kid, I've got a veil full of pissed off ghosts you do not want to meet.

Beard tucks both hands into his jeans. I grab a cigarette, a real fucking smoke, out of my pocket and light up while I wait on a counter-offer. The smoke makes my stomach rumble, a bodily message that nicotine is not a Philly cheesesteak.

"I'll give you two-hundred bucks," Beard says.

"Deal."

Beard digs into his pocket and takes out a bankroll of cash. This is why I hate negotiating. As long as I've been around, you'd think I'd be good at it. Beard peels off two hundred-dollar bills and hands them to me.

"Pleasure doing business with you," Beard says.

Slick smiles like a court jester and throws his leg over the bike. He revs the engine full to redline.

I nod and head back for Second Life. Fox is inside, she's already got two outfits slung across her arm. One is a pair of black slacks and a blouse of cherry blossoms. On top of that is a pair of jeans and a Bad Religion t-shirt.

"How'd it go?" Fox eyes a row of different color Chucks.

"Well enough. I got some cash for some clothes and a couple sandwiches."

Fox licks her lips. "I am *starving*. Hurry up."

My stomach rolls. Shopping is easy enough. I grab a pair of slacks, a long sleeve button up, and a vest. The vest is a size too big, but its got a cinch at the back. My shoes are still neat enough. I meet Fox at the register. She's added a pair of llama-print socks and black sneakers.

The cashier, a bored guy in eyeliner with half his head shaved, rings us up without a word. He pauses as he rings up the blouse to eye Fox. Finishing his silent judgement, he tosses our stuff in a bag.

"One-fifty and thirty-six cents," the cashier says.

I hand him the hundreds and he makes our change.

"Can we use your changing room?"

"Sure."

Fox and I get changed and head over to the sub shop. I eat enough cheesesteak to clog all my major arteries and Fox has a chicken parmesan. We split a basket of fries the size of a volleyball.

"You ready to get this over with?"

Fox sighs. "Do we have to?"

"No. We don't."

Vampire Valley

Fox takes my hand. "Thank you," she says quietly.

I squeeze her palm in mine. She takes one deep breath and pushes up from our booth.

Chapter 22

Out front we pass a pair of couples on their way into the sub shop.

"I think she's an inspiration," a sharp woman covered in robes says.

"Out to help everyone. She speaks for the masses," this from a guy who is one letterman's jacket away from his glory years. "It's just politician BS. Worse, that lady and her dad aren't even politicians, just rich folk."

Letterman's girlfriend, a girl covered in tattoos that could be a stone, punches his arm. "Don't be a dick, Bradley. Besides, Sarah is like, young. I bet if she takes over there's going to be parties like every night."

Definitely a stone.

The stone nudges the sharp with his elbow. The sharp awkwardly leans into her boyfriend, the most standard looking standard I've seen today.

The party passes into the restaurant. The closed door cuts off their chatter.

"Win or lose," I say, "Sarah's making an impression."

"We've lived down here in the Glow long enough to know people are desperate for a change. These people need something to believe in. Sarah is giving that to them."

"You sound like you're starting to believe. All that talk of recruiting getting to you?"

"I can think of worse things than two women running the city." Fox's phone chirps.

She holds a finger up to wait and digs out her phone. I watch as the color drains from her face.

"What is it?"

She hands the phone to me. It's a picture of Jordon, tied to a chair with an anti-shifting symbol burned into his neck. The room is empty, but a small window over his left shoulder looks out into an alley. Something about the picture scratches at the back of my brain. Why do I know this?

"The fuck?" I click out of the picture. It came attached to the message: We will remove a limb every time Sarah goes on TV.

Unknown number.

"What the hell is this?" I ask.

"Someone's not happy about a woman running the city." Fox clicks around on her phone. "I'm going to send this to Ethan. Maybe his people can find something about the number or the picture."

"What do we do now?"

"We go to the news station," Fox says.

Not the answer I expected. "You sure?"

"Yes. For one, Sarah might have more information."

"Are you going to try and stop her from going on tonight?"

Fox's lip curls. She shakes her head. "Whoever has Jordon is going to do whatever they are going to do regardless. If they are trying to stop Sarah, she's probably doing something right. If Ethan texts me back and says to do something about Sarah, we'll re-evaluate. The best thing we can do for Jordon is find out who has him."

It's a cold statement, but she's right. Since I looked at the message, one name has been playing in my head, Burgess. He has the most to gain from silencing Sarah.

I throw my leg over the Bonneville.

Fox clears her throat. "You gave yours away. Either steal another one or you're riding bitch."

A quick glance of the lot shows nothing worth stealing. After watching Fox scrape pegs the whole way here, riding on the back is a terrifying concept. I'm too tired to argue. I slide onto the back seat.

Fox gets on the bike in front of me. "Give me a kick?"

I syphon off a touch of magic. In my head, I picture the engine turning over. I give the engine a mental kick and it fires to life.

Fox clicks the bike into gear and tears out of the parking lot. The drive is less ass-clenching than expected. Fox obeys the traffic laws, to some extent. No splitting lanes or dragging pegs. I'm not sure if she's worried or thinking or what. When this is over, I'm taking her so far away from all this bullshit.

At the edge of the Glow, I catch a glimpse of a car in the side mirror. The car is remarkable in its unremarkability. Cars in the Glow are as loud as its inhabitants. They are flashy or primered or broke down or just plain noisy. The car in the mirror is a beige sedan, new but not brand new. I glance over my shoulder and the car is gone.

My gaze drifts to the mirror constantly for the rest of the ride, but I don't see the car again.

Fox parks in front of the news station. The lot is full of cars ranging from broke-ass-intern-shitboxes to a look-at-me green Audi R8 that I guarantee belongs to O'Malley.

Inside, a pleasant receptionist asks us why we're there and points us down a hall when we tell her. The hall leads us to a dressing room.

Sarah's inside, a pair of women working on her hair and make-up. She smiles at Fox. "Hey, I'm so glad you made it."

"Did you talk to Lily?" Fox places her hands on her hips.

"Are you okay?" Sarah sits forward in her chair. She shoos away the estheticians.

Fox shows Sarah her phone. Sarah's hand rises to a nautilus pendant hanging by her throat.

"That's the kidnapped hair?"

"His name is Jordon." Fox puts her phone away. "Did you talk to Lily?"

Sarah crosses the room to close her dressing room door. "Yes. Lily said that Darius has been acting strange."

"Strange how?" I ask. Sharps are strange at the best of times.

"Lily told me Darius has been increasingly paranoid. He thinks one of the elders is about to rise against him."

"Sounds like normal sharp shit," I say. "Coups are their MO. They're due."

Sarah shrugs. "Whatever it is this time, it's got Darius spooked."

Fox paces the room. "Okay, Darius is spooked. How does that link to everything going on in Hair Nation?"

"It might be nothing, but..." Sarah trails off.

"But what?" Fox's voice is harsh. She doesn't play games and the look on her face says she doesn't enjoy being led by Sarah.

"Darius has been trying to find allies outside of the valley," Sarah says. "The word is, Burgess has been hiring up sharps left and right lately. He's even hired a sharp lawyer a while back."

Sharp lawyers are a thing. All the warding to protect them from magic keeps people from trying to alter negotiations or contracts with magic.

"So," I say, "Darius is looking for friends and Burgess is suddenly on a sharp hiring spree. Do you think Burgess would buddy up with Darius?"

"Lloyd would do anything if he thought he had something to gain from it."

I roll the plot around in my head. Darius needs friends, Burgess obliges, never hurts to have an old sharp in your back pocket. The old man is having a hard time burying Ethan in the public eye, that charming old hound has the hearts and loins of half the city. Burgess hires sharps to attack the alpha.

Then Sarah goes nightly-news-official with her down-with-Burgess campaign. He sees Fox on the news with Sarah, knows Fox has a connection with the hairs. Has Darius pick up a hostage to try and scare Fox and the hairs off of backing Sarah?

That's one hell of a yarn. Is it true? It's definitely plausible. This is why I've stayed away from politics for hundreds of years. This shit is treacherous and you never know who your friends are. Everyone uses each other, and no one has any damn loyalty.

"What are you going to do?" Sarah asks.

"Find Jordon. That's first. We can deal with power players later. I just need to make sure the kid is safe."

Sarah nods. "Send me that picture. I'll put some people on it and see if they can find anything."

Fox clicks around on her phone to forward the message.

A heavy fist pounds on the door. Fox and I jump. Silver flashes in her grip as I reach for the magic revolver.

"Easy," Sarah says. "It's just Kylee."

Sarah opens the door. A large troll stands outside, she's wearing a headset and holding a clipboard that looks like a children's toy in her hands.

"Hello, Ms. Roswell," Kylee says. "They need you on set in five."

"Thank you so much, Kylee." Sarah smiles and touches the back of Kylee's hand. "I'll be ready. Will you send Ashleigh and Hailee back in for me?"

Kylee smiles. "Yes, Ms. Roswell." She nods and steps back into the hall.

"Do you need me out there with you?" Fox asks.

Sarah sits back in the dressing room chair and smiles at Fox. "You don't have to be on stage, but they said I could have one guest just off camera. I was hoping that would be you."

"Oh," Fox says. "Okay."

"You are the strongest woman I've ever met. It means a lot to have you in my corner."

"Uh, yeah. Sure." Fox stumbles.

Sarah says, "There's a viewing area behind the cameramen. Sam, you're welcome to watch from there. Wish me luck." Sarah speaks to us from the mirror. The bright lights make her pale complexion almost ghostly, fitting for an all-powerful necromancer, I suppose. I look at myself in the mirror. Am I that pale? There's nothing but a tired guy in a cheap vest staring back at me.

"Break a leg."

Chapter 23

Fox finds her way to a quiet corner of the set. I climb a couple stairs to a viewing area behind the cameras.

O'Malley is already set up, centered behind a desk with enough to make room for the egos of all parties—it's a big fucking desk. A well-dressed guy applies the final touches of make-up to the host.

A whole crew of producers and cameramen are between the stage and me, but the viewing platform is elevated enough that I can see. Sarah exits a room on the left and takes a seat at the news desk. She smiles over her shoulder at Fox, before turning back to face the cameras. O'Malley shuffles through notecards, gives fuck all about Sarah's presence. She says something to him, too quiet to hear. Prick doesn't answer.

Sarah stiffens in her chair, steals another glance over her shoulder. Fox forces a stiff smile. She keeps moving her hands.

Lily and Magnus, Sarah's pet sharp and mage, file in next to me. We exchange awkward greetings and fall into an awkward silence.

"Live in three," someone near the stage calls out.

O'Malley sips his water, clears his throat. He's still yet to acknowledge the 'guest' to his right. I wonder if this is how he treated Ethan a few days ago. Probably worse. Sarah is at least rich; Ethan's just a hair.

At the one-minute warning, Burgess appears from the right. A female mage in full body armor and a long black hair braided with military precision joins him. The holster at her hip is empty. At least the news station disarmed the mage, not like she needs lead to punch holes in shit. Fox eyes the mage from the opposite side of the set, scoffs.

I open my mind to the magic in the air, not grabbing at the energy, just putting out mental feelers. The atmosphere tastes bitter and angry with more than a hint of fear. The energy shifts toward Magnus and Lloyd's bodyguard. Neither are being particularly discrete about gobbling up the magic like hungry fucking hippopotami. I sip on the energy, trying to focus on the fear.

Magnus glances at me, something like amusement written on the lines of his face. His cold blue eyes take me in, blonde beard spotted with gray pulls back as he smiles. It's the kind of expression a parent gives a kid's macaroni art. Great job, Sammy Boy. Now fuck off, daddy's talking to his grown-up friends.

Burgess takes his seat, his posture ramrod straight, and clasps his hands in his lap. O'Malley smiles like a geek and says something to Lloyd. They share a laugh that's as genuine as a fruit bowl painted by a first-year art student.

A guy at the edge of the set holds up five fingers.
Four.
Three.
Two.
One.

"Hello, O'Malley here and have I got a show in store for you tonight." O'Malley says directly into the camera. "We've got exclusive access to the hot new fad sweeping the politics of Mountain City, Sarah Roswell. Across the aisle is her father; influencer, philanthropist, advisor to the mayor, the largest employer in the city, and all-around gentleman, Lloyd Burgess."

Well, this is off to an unbiased start.

Sarah's jaw flinches as she holds her smile.

O'Malley turns to Sarah. "I'd like to start with you, Sarah. Your father has been running this city since before you were born. Under his guidance, the city is prospering. What has made you so determined to upset the status quo when the status quo seems to be working?"

"Well, sure," Sarah says. "Your 'status quo' is working great for the bureaucrats downtown, but in the Glow, Vampire Valley, Hair Nation, all over the city there's nothing but poverty and strife. I'm talking about changes that are best for the city, not just Burgess. I—"

"Well, I'm going to stop you there." O'Malley's grin is acid eating through the false smile. "The separation of the city is for everyone's own good. Wouldn't you say, Mr. Burgess?"

"You might be too young to remember..." Lloyd grins at Sarah.

To the world, Sarah's his daughter, but she's actually his wife reborn. I squeeze my fists, finding more of the fear entering into my body. Magnus glances at me again, eyebrow arched.

Lloyd is still going. "...good for everyone. Look at the Glow. You have hairs without their packs, sharps without their families, mages who are illiterate. It's a mess. Separation of powers is how we keep the city safe."

"I can't argue with that," O'Malley says. "Have you seen crime rates in the Glow? Why would we invite that to the safety of our boroughs?"

Sarah presses her palms flat on the desk. "The crime is because of the poverty." Her voice is sure, determined. "These people are struggling. We can't blame them because they didn't find a naïve girl with rich parents to con out of their fortune."

"Excuse me?" Lloyd coughs.

"You didn't have a dime, just a smile and a plan. You used my momma for her family's money."

Burgess growls. "That's preposterous. I'm a successful businessman."

Sarah sits back in her seat, smiles. "How much of your own money was used to start Burgess Inc?"

"Th-that's none..."

"How much of Grandpa's money went into Burgess Inc?"

Burgess's chin flaps as he tries to form words.

"Surely your grandparents made their investments back," O'Malley interjects, trying to salvage the interview. "A business loan paid back in full."

"Of course," Sarah says. "All I'm saying is my *father* had a chance at something most citizens of Mountain City never will, a multi-million dollar initial investment."

"So you're saying—" O'Malley starts, but Burgess cuts over him.

"Silly girl is upset over the pre-nup," Lloyd babbles.

Sarah smiles ear to ear.

"Excuse me?" Even O'Malley looks like he's gripping the desk to keep from falling off the Earth. "The what?"

Burgess takes a deep breath, pinches the bridge of his nose. "My will. She's upset because I cut her out of my will."

"But that's not what you said, Lloyd," Sarah says.

"I just got confused."

We should have brought popcorn.

"This girl," Burgess says, "she's throwing a fit over being cut out of my will. I've already spoken to my lawyer over the matter. And everything she says is non-sense, all this talk of unity. Do you know what kind of people she associates with?"

"What kind?" It's O'Malley who looks like he wants popcorn.

"Ethan Grisom, for one. The hair is an arms dealer and has a criminal record, but he's the tip of the iceberg."

Something akin to a lead weight forms in the pit of my stomach. I don't like where this is going.

O'Malley nods at one of the producers. Pictures of four women and two men pop up on the screen. Fox's jaw hangs slack, she sways on her feet.

"Claire Desjardins, twenty-eight," O'Malley says. "Garrett Smith, thirty-six. Aubrey Angles, forty-one. Andrew Dennison, twenty-two. Heather Clark, thirty."

Fox stares at her feet.

"Angie Aines, forty-seven." O'Malley puts on his best mournful face. "These are all lost souls. What can you tell me about them, Mr. Burgess?"

Sarah stares at the pictures, confused.

"These are a sampling of the poor souls my daughter's associate, Fox Flint, has left without a body. The kitsune pushed all of these folks from their bodies and then left them wandering. The woman has a trail of bloody shamblers longer than Mori Yuki."

Yuki…Where the hell do I know that name from?

"What do you say to that, Ms. Roswell?" O'Malley asks.

"It doesn't matter," Burgess says. "We have a team of officers standing by, prepared to arrest Mrs. Flint."

Movement from my left catches my eye. It's a team of four or five cops, outfitted in SWAT gear. Before I can react, a sudden whoosh of magic passes over my shoulder. Energy rushes forward. Steel snaps and light fixtures explode as a large piece of the set falls toward the stage.

Another rush of energy as Lloyd's mage slides his chair to safety. Then a sonic boom's worth of magic rushes toward the stage. The light bar hoovers, two feet above Sarah's head. O'Malleys got his head tucked under the desk like it would save him from the thousands of pounds of metal.

Whispers pass through everyone in attendance. Sarah makes a motion with her hand. A wave ripples through the air, revealing two dozen spectral entities holding up the set. Three different cameramen give themselves whiplash trying to focus on the magic.

The sound of a door closing behind me catches my attention.

Fox is already sprinting in my direction. With some luck we can catch the culprit, or at the very least allude the cops.

Chapter 24

I run up a set of steel stairs. There's a door at the top, some kind of fire exit. A small speaker blares an high-pitched alarm. I push out the door, Fox on my heels.

We exit on to the roof. Look left, nothing. Right, catch a glimpse of movement. I run after the figure. Long white hair blows in the wind as they leap to the next rooftop over.

The gap from this building to the next is an easy ten feet. I stop at the edge to survey the jump. The other building is a story lower. I could probably—

Fox blows past me, making the jump without a flinch. She lands on her feet and rolls across the other building. Fuck.

I back up and get a running start. Some of the energy from the studio is still in the tanks, I give a little boost. The spell isn't perfect, and I end up launching myself ten feet too far. I land next to Fox who is already up and running, tumbling head over heels before getting my feet back under me.

The white-haired assailant is already to the far end of this building. He's not wearing a shirt and blue lines of magical energy weave down his spine like a corset. What the fuck am I chasing?

Without a glance back, the man drops off the edge of the roof. Fox and I make to the ledge a moment later.

"Do you seem him?" Fox huffs between breaths.

The alley below is empty. He didn't have time to enter any of the doors; he's just gone. I shake my head and try to catch my breath. Fox throws her leg over the edge, but I set a hand on her shoulder.

"Let him go. We have bigger problems than some lunatic taking pot shots at Sarah."

Fox grits her teeth, doesn't give chase. My phone buzzes in my pocket. I ignore the phone and hope Fox can't hear the sound over the din of the city. The last thing she needs is to be worried about a prank phone call. I can check the message later.

I take Fox by the hand and lead her to a fire escape on the opposite side of the building. The two of us climb down. Three high class SUVs haul ass away from the new studio. My guess is Burgess high-tailing it. Instinctively, I draw off the energy. Can I open the veil wide enough for three SUVs to pass through? Garage door to the underworld. As I focus on the veil, a shout snaps my concentration.

"Fox!" Sarah waves a hand from the front of the studio. "I'm so glad you're okay." She jogs up to us and wraps Fox into a hug.

Fox eyes me over Sarah's shoulders. She mouths, "What the fuck?"

I clear my throat. Sarah steps back from the hug and looks us both over. "Are you both okay?"

"Yeah, fine," Fox says.

"We tried to chase them." I light up two cigarettes, pass one to Fox. The chase and the energy I syphoned off have me keyed up. If I can't blow off the feelings, at least I can keep my hands busy.

Fox takes a smoke with a quiet, "Thank you."

"They were too quick," I say. "Any idea what the fuck that was about?"

Sarah shakes her head. She glares in the direction of the Burgess's motorcade. "Had to be Lloyd." For the first time, I notice a thick vein running down the middle of Sarah's forehead. It pulses with her racing heartbeat.

Am I hyped up from my actions or because Sarah is? That's a tomorrow kind of question. I file it away under 'shit I never want to know about the deal I made with the devil'.

"I'm not sure it was Burgess," I say.

"What makes you say that?"

Sarah and Fox both look at me expectantly.

"Lloyd's mage was surprised. She didn't react until after the metal started falling. If it was a con job, the mage would have been quicker on the trigger."

Sarah stares after Burgess.

Another SUV pulls up. Magnus steps out of the front passenger door and opens the rear. Lily is behind the wheel, still covered in tactical gear.

"It's fine, Magnus. I'll drive myself home. I want you and Lily to reach out to your contacts, find out who did this."

Magnus's gaze darts to Fox and I and back to Sarah. "Ma'am, are you sure?"

"Yes. I'm *fucking* sure. Somebody tried to kill me."

"But, ma'am—"

Sarah waves her hand. In a flash, Magnus's mouth is nothing but solid flesh. The mage's eyes go wide as Sarah, half his size, grabs him by the throat and slams him against the side of the vehicle. The back of his head shatters the front passenger window glass. She presses harder, bending the mage over backward into the SUV.

Rage boils in my chest. Pure fucking fury. I haven't felt this kind of anger since I was helpless, watching Sarah continually kill me in hopes I'd find my spine. My heart races in my chest.

"I *pay* you, both of you," Sarah's voice is a whisper of death and the promise of agony, "to keep me safe. You both failed. I cannot look after this city if I'm busy watching over my shoulder. You need to be there for me. Watch over me so I can look over the city. Do you understand?"

Magnus blows snot out of his nose. He mentally claws at the air, trying to find energy to fight back. Sarah's vacuum on the magic is all-encompassing. Magnus couldn't summon enough magic to blow out a birthday candle. He nods in agreement.

Sarah leans into his ear, whispers one final threat. She lets Magnus go and the mage drops to his ass with his back against the car door. His mouth is back and he's gasping for air.

The driver's door slams. Lily rounds the car and helps a coughing Magnus to his feet. The mage shoves away from the sharp.

"We will turn the city upside down in search of answers," Lily says. Her voice is obedient like an attack dog not fully trained. Sure, the dog will sit on command, but it's also waiting for you to fuck up so it can take your throat.

"Thank you, Lily." Sarah sits in the driver's seat. She shifts the car into gear. Out the busted window she says, "When you find them, bring them to me alive. I want to make them pay, personally."

Flashes of torture techniques that went out of style with the Crusades flash through my mind. Lots of fire and pointy objects and screaming. So much screaming. I blink away the images. Was that a glimpse into Sarah's mind? Or am I filling in her intentions with my own memories?

"Fox, I'll be in touch when I know our move. And I'll let you know if I hear anything about your young hair."

"Thank you," Fox says.

Sarah pulls into traffic. Lily disappears into a crowd of people like she was never there. Magnus straightens his clothes, gives Fox and I a glare, and walks toward the Glow.

"What do we do now?" Fox asks.

"We need to get up to Hair Nation, ASAP," I say.

"Really? I figured that'd be the last place you want to be."

I sigh. It is the last place I want to be. "We don't know if Burgess was bluffing. If there's a warrant out for your arrest, we're safer in Hair Nation than anywhere else. The hairs will protect you and cops won't go up there."

Fox pulls me in for a hug. "About that—"

"That was before. It doesn't matter."

Fox and I are both old, we've both lived more lifetimes than almost anyone. When we got married, we made an agreement we'd never ask about life before each other. I don't care what happened before we met. It doesn't matter.

"Come on. We've got to get out of here."

I lead us over to a silver Nissan, some new-ish mid-level sedan. With a touch of magic, I pop the locks and open the door for Fox. She slides into the passenger seat. Another hint of magic starts the engine. Fox stares out the window, lost in some faraway thought. I slide my phone out of my pocket and feel Sarah's rage all over again when I read the message.

I won't miss next time.

Alexander Nader

Chapter 25

Traffic downtown is a bitch. The sun has set, the business crowd moved out and the nightlife crowd moved in. A sea of boring ass sedans clog all the lanes. An occasional sports car revs their engine, enlarging the owners dick and/or breast size by at least three measurements with every exhaust flame spewing backfire.

Women drunk on daiquiris hang on the arms their boyfriends, all Todds and Tuckers from accounting. Dudes three years into their ten-year plans of climbing the executive ladder. If they play best boy long enough, their bosses might pat them on the heads with enough of a raise to buy Mikayleigh or Ashleigh or Madison a rock big enough to pay for deposit on a new place after the divorce.

All I want to do is get home. Or to Hair Nation, I guess. Is that home now?

Fox has her phone connected to the car's radio. The speakers light up with the chime of an incoming call. I don't recognize the number on the screen. Fox sighs, clicks the green 'answer' button.

"Is that you, Mariko?" Fox's mother's voice comes over the speakers.

"What do you want, Hisa?"

"I saw the news earlier. They have your picture all over." She gives a weak gasp of astonishment. "It's just terrible what they're doing to you."

"And how, exactly, did the police find out about those people?" Fox's voice is sharp enough to cut diamonds.

I hadn't thought about it, hadn't had time to process, but she's right. Burgess has a lot of money but digging up that kind of information on Fox's past, that fast, seems unlikely. Does Fox think her mom is working with the old man? Is she?

There's a silence at the end of the line. Finally, her mom says, "I don't know anything about that. It seems you have made some very resourceful enemies in this town, dear."

"What do you want?"

"It's time to come home. The authorities are looking for you. It's dangerous here."

"I'm not scared of some cops," Fox says.

"It's not just the police. There are darker things out there. All this attention might summon the—"

"Don't you threaten me with that boogeyman. She's just a scary story you told me to keep me in line. I'm not a child anymore."

"You don't believe because you were raised in the shelter of the palace. Believe in the Piper, or not, all the same she will come for you if she thinks you've gone ronin."

"Is this really all you wanted? To scare me with stories?"

"What I want is to take you home. I have a suitable host for you. Yuuka has come all this way to pledge herself the kitsune."

What the hell does that mean?

"Do you want to dishonor her and her family by sending her away?"

Fox punches the dash. "Don't you fucking put this on me. I didn't ask for this, any of it." She sniffs back tears.

"It doesn't matter—"

I press a button on the steering wheel, ending the call. Fox curls her feet up into the seat. I take her hand, it's cold and sweaty. That phone call wrecked my wife in a way I've never seen. Half the words are lost on me. I don't know jack shit about Kitsune culture and I'm learning bits and pieces with every run in with Fox's mom.

Suitable host? What does that mean?

We ride in bumper-to-bumper silence for a while. How do I console Fox after that mess? Deciding on a prompt change of subject, I say something that's been scratching at the back of my head for an hour now.

"Who is Mori Yuki?"

A group of drunk stones pass in front of the car, cutting over to a bar on the other side of the street. Fox watches them cross before answering.

"You don't remember?"

"The name rings a bell, but I can't place it."

"He was a masochist and a serial killer, sort of."

The words bring back a flood of media coverage. I remember now. Mori Yuki was a kitsune serial killer. He roamed all over but had a taste for the southern states. The guy was all kinds of fucked up, obsessed with pain. Mori would share a body with his victims and try to see how much pain they could take before their soul left their body. A kitsune, like Fox, could push a soul out without much effort, but that wasn't for Mori. He wanted to put them through so much anguish they vacated their own body. The creepy fucker got off on the pain.

He left a trail of bloody shamblers, bodies without souls, in his wake that stretched from Miami to Houston and back again. It's fuzzy now, but I think they caught him somewhere in West Virginia, the serial killer who flew too close to Quantico. There was a big hullabaloo around the trial and execution. First, he hadn't *technically* killed anyone, just caused so much pain their souls left their own bodies. Second, how would they deal with the execution since he was still in the body of one of his victims.

"Fuck," I say. "That guy."

"Yeah," Fox says. "That guy."

"Fuck those media assholes," I say. Angry all over again.

Fox shakes her head. Her red hair falls over the side of her face, obscuring her expression.

"Seriously, those pieces of shit don't know anything about you."

"That's very kind, but you don't know me."

"You're my wife. Of course, I know you."

"You don't know me from before."

"I know you now, and that's good enough."

We ride in silence for another few moments. When will this fucking traffic break? I never thought I'd be so anxious to get back to hair country.

"It's true, you know," Fox says.

"What is?"

"All those people. I did that to them, left them as shamblers."

"I'm sure you had your reasons," I say.

Fox sniffles again. "They were bitch reasons."

"Reasons none the less."

"I was running. Running from her."

"Your mom?"

"Yeah. I ran away from home. She's been chasing me ever since. Every time I caught someone looking at me weird or saw a person I thought might be one of her guards, I jumped ship. Those people on the TV, they were only a sample of the shamblers I left behind." Fox knocks her head into the window.

I squeeze her thigh. "How long were you running?"

"Long before my people ever decided siding with the Germans was a good idea."

Shit.

I knew Fox was old, but I don't know that I expected that. Christ. How long was she running? A hundred years? A century of jumping from body to body, always looking over her shoulder. That sounds like torture.

"Whatever happened before now, before a year ago," I say, "before right this fucking moment doesn't matter. You're my wife and you don't have to run from a goddamn thing ever again in your life." I kiss the back of her hand. "I've got you."

Fox leans across the car and rests her head on my shoulder. She hitches with shuddering breaths before easing into a steady rhythm.

Traffic backs off. We push past the boundaries of Downtown and into the no man's land between the end of Downtown and the start of Hair Nation.

Thank god. I ease onto the accelerator as a group of ten motorcycles blows by in the other lane, angry v-twins rattling my brain. It's only a couple miles to the edge of hairitory. We are home free. The digital speed on the dash settles on five over the limit, just enough to keep from drawing attention from the cops.

Just as Fox's body goes slack with exhaustion, blue lights flash in my mirror.

Chapter 26

Fuck every single fucking thing that is holy. I debate stomping on the accelerator. It's only a couple miles to hair town. The cops probably won't follow. Or will they? Shit, like it matters. I'm in an econobox. The cops with their Hemis would run circles around my ass.

Shit.

I draw on the energy in the air. It tastes like panic. My own damn panic flavoring the magic. Calm down, take it easy. I focus on slowing my heart rate, put on my blinker.

The siren chirps a couple times to let me know they're serious.

Shit. Shit, shit, shit.

The magic still feels weird, but I take in as much as I can. I focus on crafting the most standard of all standards in my head. He's a guy, not tall, not short. The guy has brownish, blondish hair, short cropped. He's average weight. His eyes might be green or blue, depends on the lighting. With everything in my heart, I cast that projection onto Fox.

"Wait, huh?" Fox, standard ass Fox, sits up. She glances in the mirror. "Shit."

"I think I cast a decent glamour. Play it cool and we'll be fine." I edge onto the shoulder.

The tires rumble over gravel and then onto grass. The road is two lanes, but the shoulder is wide enough for passing cars to have plenty of room.

A trillion-lumen spotlight shines in my side mirror. The light reflects back and blinds me. The light shifts as a large figure gets out of the passenger side of the car. Another, smaller figure exits the driver's side. Both approach the car with hands on their holsters.

Shit.

The normal sized cop stands next to my window. His thumb flips the clasp holding his gun loose. "License and registration." His body blocks most of the light so I can get a good look at him.

The cop is older, late forties. His face is all mustache and tired lines from too long on the job. There's a tension in his movements, like he's itching for something to pop off.

"Is there something wrong, officer?" I try to sound calm, keep my focus on the Fox's illusion.

The car tilts to the right as the cop's partner, an old troll, rests his weight on Fox's door. Gray skin of the troll's belly peeks out from under his shirt. The troll scratches at his belly button before his hand rests back on a comically large gun. I've never seen a troll use a gun before, but the thing looks modified to fit the creature's oversized grip.

"License and registration," standard cop repeats.

I hold my hands up. No sudden movements. "I'm reaching for my documentation, okay?"

The cop blows air out his mustache-hole. That's code speak for affirmative.

I lean across the car and grab the first two slips of paper my hands land on. Using the same glamour I'm casting on Fox, I change the papers to be the proper documentation. Car and insurance registered to James Harlow. I pass the papers to the cop and reach for my wallet in my back pocket.

"Whoa." Standard Cop draws his gun. "What are you doing?"

"Sorry," I say. "Sorry. I was just reaching for my license."

"Do it slow," he says. He's got his 9mm trained on me now and it's not going anywhere.

"Why don't you take it easy with the gun, hoss," Dude-Fox says. Their voice has the faint hint of a guy born in the south but trying hard to hide their accent.

"No one was talking to you," Troll Cop says.

"No one appreciates your shakedowns," Fox says, "but here we are."

"It's fine Fo—" Shit. Think fast. "Fozzy. It's fine, Fozzy."

Standard Cop laughs. "Fozzy?"

"Old nickname." I take my license out, pass a quick glamour over the name, and hand it to Standard Cop.

The cop doesn't so much as glance at the documentation. "I'm going to need you to step out of the car."

"Why?" I fire back.

"Get out of the car." Standard Cop's gun is still hanging in my face, a silent threat.

"Why don't you—" Fox starts.

"It's okay, *Fozzy*," I say. "We've done nothing wrong." Slowly, I reach for the door.

Standard Cop takes a step back to allow me to open the door. I ease out of the car. The cop grabs me by the shoulder and pushes me against the car. I want to deck the guy, rage and tell him to get his hands off me, but it doesn't matter. Play it cool. They can't see Fox, my documentation checks out. This will all be over soon.

"You, too," the troll grunts at Fox.

I can't see Dude-Fox glowering at the troll, but I can see Dude-Fox glowering at the troll. The door pops open and Fox, still looking like an average dude, steps out. The troll grabs them and spins them against the car. Fox grunts as the troll puts his club hand against their back.

"Hey, hold still," Standard Cop says to Fox.

"I am holding—"

Troll Cop slams Fox's face against the roof of the car. The sheet metal dents under her head. Her eyes dart side to side, unfocused as blood drips from her nostril.

Oh, fuck this.

"What the hell is wrong with you?" I push back from the car, but Standard Cop drives his arm into my back.

"Stop resisting," he says.

"I'm not resis—" My muscles clench and my skin tingles as an electric current runs through my body.

Standard Cop keeps the taser running until my muscles are jelly under my skin. My legs buckle and I collapse to the ground.

I hear Fox—she's real Fox now, the shock broke my concentration on the spell—scream.

"Get your hands off of me."

"Stop resisting."

I hear gravel being kicked. The Standard Cop yelps with pain. "You bitch," he shouts. My legs refuse to respond to my commands. I'm begging for them to move. Pleading. With everything in my will, I ache to stand up, to come to Fox's rescue. She needs me.

Figures pass in front of me. I turn on my back to see Troll Cop. He's got his arms hooked around behind Fox in a full-nelson. A blade shines in one of her hands, but it's flailing helplessly over her head.

"Get off me," Fox screams.

Standard cop trains his gun on Fox's chest. He looks at me. "Burgess wants you to know you did this to yourself." He turns back to Fox.

I claw at any energy I can wrap my mind around. My brain is too panicked and scrambled to conjure any kind of particular focus. I swipe my hand through the air, praying it's enough to disturb the veil.

A wave the size of a stage curtain ripples through the air.

"What the…?" Troll Cop shuffles backward, away from the ripple. He drops Fox and draws his sidearm.

Standard Cop turns to come face to face with a ghost stone. The ghost has spiked hair and his right arm is solid rock. The ghost screeches loud enough to shatter the car windows as it swings the club at Standard Cop. He doesn't have the time to react before the ghost cracks his skull with a solid stone right hook.

Troll Cop pops off a half dozen shots as three more ghosts step through the veil.

"Fox," I yell. She scrambles to her feet and races to my side.

My legs won't respond to commands. Fox doesn't waste any time. She tosses me in the back seat, gets behind the wheel. I use the last bit of magic in me to crank the throttle. Fox jams the car in gear and burns the tires.

The car passes through two women ghosts. A chill passes down my spine as their energy touches me. The ghosts groan. I watch out the back window as they close in on Troll Cop. Muzzle flashes light up the night. The stone straddles Standard Cop. His rock hard arm slams down on the cop's head again and again.

Fox rounds a corner and I lose sight of the brouhaha. I let go of my hold on the curtain and pray it falls back into place. Something beyond exhaustion grips my mind, blackness takes hold of my soul.

Chapter 27

"Hey, Sam. You dead?" Something presses at my shoulder. "I think he's dead," the voice says.

"Shut up, Gabriel." That voice is definitely Fox. "He's fine, just tired. Help me get him to bed."

Strong arms scoop me out of the car by my arm pits. I flail out of Gabriel's grip. My legs wobble, but I catch myself on the hood of the car. The world is a blur. I blink and try to focus, try to remember why I'm so tired.

"Whoa there, killer," Gabriel says.

"What the...Did I set a bunch of ghosts on some dirty cops?" I press my palms into my eyelids, trying to get the goddamn universe to stop spinning.

Fox wraps her arm around me. "You did. My hero."

"Hey," I say. "I saved you for once."

"I had it under control."

"I know you did." The world is all blurry lights and floaters at the edges of my vision. "Where are we?"

"How fucked up are you?" Gabriel says.

"Just enough to pick a fight with a werewolf." I spin and put my hands up in front of me.

Gabriel laughs, ruffles my hair like I'm a child. "I like you, Flint. Come on. Let's get you to bed." Gabriel throws my arm over his shoulder and leads me...well, leads me somewhere.

"Wait. Fox, where are you?"

"I'll be right there." Fox's voice is somewhere behind me. "Ethan and I need to talk."

"Not without me." I shrug out from under Gabriel's arm and move toward where I heard Fox's voice.

"You need to go to bed." Fox to my left now.

I turn towards her. "You aren't getting out of my sight."

"Everything is out of your sight right now. You're blind as a bat."

She's close. I reach out and snatch a handful of air. Shit.

"Doesn't matter," I say. "I'm coming."

Fox sighs. She takes my hand, leads me across the gravel. "I should lead you into a wall for being so stubborn."

"I would walk through five hundred walls as long as I wound up at your door."

"That's not how that goes."

"It is now." I trip over my feet, catch myself. What happened to your other senses picking up when one fails?

The air smells like damp forest. My mouth tastes like sulfur. That's concerning. Fox's hand is warm in mine. All I can hear is my feet crunching on gravel and Gabriel laughing behind me.

All of that does jack shit for telling me how to keep from walking into a wall.

We pass through the door of what I'm assuming is the hairhouse of guns. The interior is quiet. The slamming door echoes through the large space. Fox turns and we walk up the stairs.

"Last one," Fox says as I get to the top step. She leads me the rest of the way to Ethan's office.

"What happened to you?" Ethan's heavy voice booms across the room.

"Me?" I say. "Nothing. I'm peachy."

After a silent moment, Fox says, "Someone went a little overboard with the magic." She directs me to the large couch.

I take a seat and stare into a halo of light coming from the ceiling. Little black filaments swim through my vision. This shit better get better soon. I've got stuff to do today.

"Uh-huh," Ethan says.

"You look better," Fox says.

"I'm starting to feel better. Most of the cuts have healed over. Definitely not a hundred percent, but I'm less of a liability. The pack isn't handling me like a house of cards."

"That's good."

The couch cushion next to me sinks. That better be Fox. A soft hand rests in mine. Definitely better be Fox.

"Any news on Jordon?" Fox says from next to me.

Thank god. That coulda been real weird.

Ethan sighs. "No. I've got all my people looking over the picture, but no one can place it. We're sure it's not in Hair Nation and there's a window in the picture so it's probably not in the valley either."

I focus on the picture in my mind, it's not like I can see anything else anyway. Jordon and that window. That damn window looking out into an alley. Where do I know that from? Somewhere. Think dammit.

The edges of the image burn away as reality sinks in. I blink my eyes and focus on the room. Fox stares into my eyes. I can't help but smile at her.

"Hello, beautiful," I say.

Ethan growls in the back of his throat, but a stern look from Fox silences the alpha.

"Welcome back," she says.

"Yeah, maybe I shouldn't do that again."

"Probably not."

"What did you do, exactly?" Ethan asks.

"You all need to see this." Elsa busts into the office and marches to the television. She grabs the remote and turns on the news.

Some blonde lady with the kind of face made for judging the poor and unfortunate souls born below her station speaks into the camera. "…details are slim, but here's what we know so far. A wanted fugitive and her husband attacked police officers during a routine stop."

"Routine my ass," I shout at the TV.

"Two officers are dead and MCPD has had to contract the Supernatural Forces Department to try and contain the ghosts currently rampaging through the city."

The news lady touches her ear. "Ladies and gentlemen, I'm being informed MCPD has provided us with bodycam footage from the incident."

"They got their hands on that awful fucking fast," I say.

"I want to warn you, this contains graphic footage and is not suitable for sensitive viewers."

The screen cuts to a choppy image from Standard Cop approaching my car. "License and registration, sir."

"The fuck?" I say.

The audio has been edited. All of the tension, the electricity in the air is gone. It's been dubbed over with a cool, calm cop. Probably from some other traffic stop.

"Why?" The recording of me snaps back.

"That's not right," I say. "I didn't snap until he told me to get out of the car for no fucking reason."

The body cam jump cuts. I'm chest first against the car. "What the hell is this?" My body spins. The camera goes black. Subtitles on the screen read: The mage appears to have tried to destroy the video evidence.

"You fuckers want to talk about doctoring footage," I yell at the TV. I have to fight the urge to jump up and down on the couch and shout.

Fox squeezes my hand, a silent 'take it easy, hon'.

"Stop resisting," Standard Cop shouts. Then, "I said to stop resisting…what are you?...oh god…no." The black screen video concludes with the clubbing thud of a ghost stone knocking someone dead.

"Fuck," I say under my breath.

The news lady comes back on screen, her stone face set to something close to mournful. "Officer Pillman and Office Austin each leave behind wives and children." She clears her throat. "The assailants have connections to Sarah Roswell, daughter of philanthropist Lloyd Burgess. Fox Flint is currently wanted due to breaking several counts of Yuki's Law. Her husband, Samuel Flint, is wanted for the murders of Officers Pillman and Austin. These two individuals are considered very dangerous. If you see them, call the police immediately. Do not—"

Ethan switches off the television.

"That's not how it happened," I say. "Tell them Fox."

Ethan gives a dismissive wave. "You don't have to tell me what it's like to make an enemy of Burgess. Do you think these tactics are new?"

They're new to me, but this probably isn't the crowd to bring that up to. I think about the hairs at the police station, arrested for minor offenses. The standards who started the problems let go with a slap on the wrist. Maybe Sarah is right, this town does need a change in leadership.

"Fuck Burgess," is the best I can manage.

"I'll drink to that." Ethan holds up a beer.

Holy hell I could use a drink. Ever since the thing with Sarah, I've felt oddly level without any alcohol, but that was 'all powerful he's got shit figured out' Sam Flint. 'Enemy of the state' Sam Flint could really use a barrel of three hundred proof.

"Y'all got any deer piss?" I ask.

"You've already gone blind once tonight," Fox says. "Do you really want to try for twice?"

Ethan already has a mason jar of liquid on his desk. He takes a pull and passes the glass to me. I take a big gulp, letting the fire of the alcohol burn away all the bullshit of the day. My entire throat feels like it is under attack, but I manage to take my poison like a champ. I reach the drink out to Elsa, but Fox snatches it out of my hand.

"I thought you were worried about going blind?"

"Like I'm going to let you have all the fun." Fox slams back a shot and hands the bottle to Elsa without so much as a flinch.

We pass the bottle around until it's empty. My warm body spins around the room and for a second, I forget that every cop in Mountain City is gunning for my wife and me. For a moment, we're just a bunch of old friends talking about shit that doesn't matter to pass the time. I fight sleep like a child. Sleep means tomorrow will come and I'll have to face my problems in the light of day. My body yearns to pull Fox into an embrace and sleep forever. We can be that ancient evil that sleeps below the city, the kind parents warn their kids with to behave. Slumber eventually comes for me and I can't fight it. I fall asleep with my head on Fox's lap as she twirls my hair around her finger.

Chapter 28

The sleep is fitful. Images and thoughts race through my mind. Dreams come and go, short ads looping on repeat without ever getting to the video. Glimpses of memories tease me. Thoughts of a sadder time, a time before Fox.

A hundred deaths replay in my mind's eye. Some accidental, most not. The last death, well the last death by my own hand, plays over and over. A cheap box cutter. A trashy alley. Long vertical cuts, wrist to elbow. The pain is brief.

Fox, the woman I'd been paid to tail, steps out of a small bar. She runs up to me. My body is floating now, slowly severing ties with this life. Blood is a river through the cracked pavement. She touches my cheek and a warmth like I've never felt goes direct to my soul. Her mouth is moving, but I hear no words. She presses on my wounds, trying to staunch a bleeding that has already ended this life. A single tear rolls down her cheek.

A cheap box cutter.

A trashy alley.

A trashy alley staring at a window. A familiar window.

"Fuck." I sit straight up out of Fox's lap.

"Huh?" Fox wipes a hand across her face. "What?"

An acrid taste burns the back of my throat. I swallow it back. "I know where Jordon is."

Fox sits up straight now, looks me in the eyes. "You what?"

"That picture. I know where he is."

"We have to tell the others," Fox says.

"No."

Why did I say no? I check the room, empty. Ethan must have gone back to his place to sleep. My head pounds in time with my heartbeat. Think about it. Okay.

"Jordon is in the Glow," I say. "If we tell Ethan, he's going to send a pack strike team down there. That is *not* the kind of image the pack needs right now."

"No," Fox admits. "Not really."

"Besides, I might be wrong. I'm basing this off a memory I had a dream of. If I'm wrong, Ethan sends a small army into the Glow for no reason. If I'm right, it's just a couple sharps. We can handle a couple vampires, right?"

Fox's forehead wrinkles. "I guess."

Ethan steps into the room with two steaming cups of coffee. "Guess what?"

"Oh, coffee. Thank you." Fox reaches out to take a cup.

Ethan passes the other to me. I nod my thanks.

"I guess we'll have to get back out there and keep looking for Jordon," Fox says.

"Over my dead body," Ethan says. "The entire city is looking for you two. You'll stay here until this shit blows over."

Fox's nostrils flair. "I'll do what I please, Ethan."

Ethan takes a step toward Fox, glances at me and stops short. "I'm not trying to tell you what to do, but please. Let us keep you safe."

"It's fine," Fox says. "Sam can cast a cloaking spell and the two of us can sneak into town no big deal. Besides, I want to ask around down in the Glow. Cops in the Glow walk around with their eyes half-closed and palms wide open. They'll never try to arrest us."

"I just don't think…" Ethan stops. He sniffs the air and I swear I can see his hackles rise.

Elsa steps through the door with a grim look on her face. "This was dropped off at the edge of the property this morning." She passes a small box to Ethan.

A thin piece of twine holds a notecard to the top.

Ethan's lip curls as he slides the note free. He growls as his eyes scan the card. When he finishes, he passes the paper to Fox. I read over her shoulder.

Drop your alliance with the necromancer or it will be a whole arm next time.

What the fuck does that mean? Ethan opens the box. He grimaces and closes his eyes. I stand to see a severed finger in the box.

"Jordon's?"

"Yes," Elsa says.

Shit. If my hunch is right, we've got to get going.

"I want everyone, every member of the pack old enough to get out there looking." Ethan drops the box on his desk. "We know they aren't holding him in Vampire Valley. Focus on downtown and the Glow. He's got to be out there somewhere."

Fox takes my hand and leads me toward the exit. "We're going." She pulls me out the door without another word.

We walk down to the Mustang. I take the driver's seat and pray the ol' car still has some go left in her. The engine turns over, the steady grumble tells me she'll hold together a little while longer.

"So," Fox says. "About that cloaking spell…can you do that?"

"I sure hope so."

It's easier to concentrate while driving. I aim the mustang toward the Glow, driving at an easy speed. Pickup trucks of hair search parties blow by me, out to find their missing brethren.

The air blows through my open window. The breeze of a car and an open road fills me with possibility. I focus the world of possibilities into a specific one. Fox and I are just a couple of boring old standards, taking a road trip in our unremarkable old Subaru.

A glance in the rear view shows my bearded face, a pair of neon pink plastic sunglasses wrapped around my faces. The rumble of the Ford's V8, smooths into a well-muffled four cylinder. Fox's red hair is now blond dreadlocks, tied at the back of her head. She smiles at me.

"You look like the world's softest lumber jack," she says.

"You look like you should be selling weed brownies to tourists on the Appalachian trail."

"That's fair."

"We should skirt downtown on the way to the Glow."

Circling around downtown will take longer, but there should be less cops. With these genius disguises, we should be good.

At the edge of Hair Nation, we roll up to a line of traffic.

"What the hell?" I lean out the window to see the cause for the backup.

The hair trucks are a few cars in front of us. Traffic creeps forward, stops for a moment, creeps forward.

"I don't like this," Fox says. She tries to peer ahead.

"It's fine. No one will know it's us. We're just a couple of hikers coming back from a day in the mountains."

Fox scratches at the back of her head. I focus on the illusion. Crafting it took energy, but maintaining it is simply a matter of holding on to a mental thread.

The line edges forward, bringing us around a bend.

"Shit."

The reason for the delay comes into view. The cops have a roadblock set up. Normally, this wouldn't have me too concerned, but there's an archway over the street.

The arch is made of wood blocks, carved with sharp symbols. The runes are anti-magic and will dissolve my cheap illusion. I've seen it before when the cops were trying to cut down on drug trafficking coming out of the Glow.

"That's not good," Fox says.

"No. It's not."

Six cop cars are spread around the arch. They are checking every vehicle as it comes through. Other cops are looking up the line.

The age-old question: Do you turn around and look suspicious or try to fake straight through?

A large pickup fills my mirrors. The thing is pulled up to my bumper.

We are eight cars back from the check point.

"What are we going to do?" Fox clicks a switchblade open and closed.

"Uhhh…"

Seven cars now.

"If we're going to go, you need to do it soon."

The road has a deep ditch on either side. The archway and cop cars take up every inch of shoulder. My car is never going to get around the checkpoint. If I wait for our turn, I might be able to punch through, but they are usually prepared for those kinds of tactics. Spike strips and guns and such.

It's too late to turn around. We are close enough it would look suspicious and the cops could follow us without much issue.

A truck full of hairs passes through the checkpoint.

Six cars.

"I don't know," I say.

"Do you think you can hold the spell through the gate?"

I shake my head. "No way."

"What about the veil?"

"What about it?"

"You've been pulling it back to let ghosts in," Fox says. "Do you think you could open the veil wide enough for us to drive through, then come out again on the other side?"

"Huh."

That's a great question. The ghost on the other side don't care much for the living, but these cops aren't going to care much for two fugitives who killed two of their brethren.

I check my mirror. The grill of a pickup truck stares back. We inch forward.

Five cars.

Now or never.

I reach out for energy. There's no point in being discrete, this has got to happen fast. I think about the veil, keeping drawing from the well. This has to go right.

The car in front of us pulls forward.

Four cars.

I leave a gap, ready to punch it through the hole as a soon as the veil opens. My mind feels like a lightning storm as I gather the energy. So far, I've only parted the curtain. I need to roll the thing up like a garage door.

My eyes flick to the rear view one last time.

I'm so focused on sucking up energy and opening a portal to the other side, I don't notice the other mage until it's too late.

A sonic boom of energy breaks my concentration. A glimpse of an energy ball to my left catches my eye. I step on the gas. The car jumps forward, rear ending the car in front of me as the pickup on my bumper explodes sky high.

Chapter 29

The carcass of the pickup truck slams roof-first in the ditch to my right. The driver's door is collapsed like it got hit be a train.

I open my door and take cover behind the passenger fender of the mustang, now back to normal. I've got no time to worry about holding threads of the illusion.

The cops scramble for cover. All guns are aimed in the direction of the blast.

A familiar old man stands twenty feet out in a field. He vacuums energy up from all around. His long white hair whips around his face as he summons a small tornado and pushes it toward the cops. They open a useless volley of rounds at the mage.

Energy surges as the mage puts up a shield that blocks the bullets. The tornado inches closer and Mountain City's finest bail to take cover in the ditch.

The mage turns his attention toward me.

He's shirtless, the same mage from the rooftops. Thick bands of magical energy are weaved from his crotch to his neck. The magic sewing job holds the man, who I ripped in half, together.

"Is that Bartholomew?" Fox peeks through the passenger window at the mage.

"It would appear so."

"How is he alive?"

I shrug. "He did say he was immortal. I'm guessing it has something to do with that."

"Sam Flint," Bartholomew yells. "I told you I was coming."

All the weird ass phone calls. It must have been good ol' Bart.

Bartholomew walks closer. He's sucking in energy with every step, building up for another attack.

"You going to do anything about this?" Fox has her orange katana at her side, but Bartholomew is never going to get close enough for it to matter.

Of all the races in Mountain City, mages are the squishiest. They learn early on to stay well away from the action.

I've still got a million watts of juice running through my body from preparing to open the curtain. Okay. I try to focus on the veil. Aiming at the spot next to Bartholomew, I pull back the veil.

Bartholomew waves a hand through the air, snapping it shut.

Well, shit.

That's fine. No big deal. I got this. There's still a well of magic in the reserves.

"It's going to take more than that, Flint," Bartholomew yells. He draws more power.

"I'm going to draw his attention," I say to Fox.

She nods.

I stay low and crab walk to the next car closest to the checkpoint. The air behind me smells like gasoline. The flipped truck leaks fluids into the grass.

Bartholomew is still drawing energy. I peek over the trunk as the mage sends a burst of air at me like a canon. I duck, stick my head between my legs.

"Shit, shit, shit," I say on repeat. Using the last of what's left in my tank, I focus on protection.

A sphere of safety forms around me as the blast of air hits the car. The vehicle slams into my shield and rolls over the top, landing in the ditch next to the truck. I'm standing exposed between my mustang and an old SUV. Fox is nowhere in sight.

Bartholomew walks closer. He's fifteen feet out now. I drop the shield and scramble for cover behind the SUV. Hopefully, Bartholomew will take shots at it instead of my car. The off-road vehicle has chest high tires. The large gap between the car and the road doesn't offer shit in the way of cover.

I peek under the Jeep and spot Bartholomew's legs. He's on the other side now.

"How are you here?" I ask.

"I'd think you, of all people, would understand the word immortal." Bartholomew's voice moves toward the rear bumper.

I sneak forward. "What's with the magic corset?"

"Apparently, stealing the life force of an immortal doesn't give the rebirth effect that you possess."

He can't die, but he can't fix himself either. Getting ripped in half must have been a real damper on his plans.

I round the front of the Jeep and check underneath for a bead on the mage. No sign of him. That can't be good. A rush of energy behind me signals an incoming attack. I dive to the side as another blast from above slams into the Jeep. The huge tires pop and the shocks blow out from the force, leaving the SUV squatting on the cracked asphalt.

Bartholomew draws more power. He's closer to the gate now. I try to draw some energy, but Bartholomew fights me. He's strong, stronger than the mages from Hair Nation the other night. I took it from them like candy from children. Bartholomew is better. We play a magical tug of war.

The fight is even, neither of us gaining any ground.

Fox pops out from behind the car closest to the gate. Her katana slashes through the air. The mage deflects the blade with a small shield, but the shift in concentration is enough. I gobble up a charge of energy and fire off a blast.

There's no time to form any kind of malice in the charge, but the energy shoves him backward enough to pass through the anti-magic arch the cops set up.

The blue laces holding him together dissolve as the two halves of Bartholomew fall to the ground. I run around the contraption. Bartholomew screams out in pain as blood and organs leak out of his broken body. He's scrabbling at the magic, but I easily take it out from under him. The pain of being ripped in half, again, is too strong for him to concentrate on magic.

After a moment of struggling, Bartholomew realizes he's not going to win the battle of magical wills. He stops the mental struggle and his body stills. The split of his body isn't perfectly symmetrical, his head ended up all on one side with the other being only the shoulder down. He stares up at me, a smile on his bloody lips.

"I can't die," he says.

"I can't leave you alone," I say.

"Clearly two pieces isn't enough." Fox sheathes her sword and draws a switchblade.

I set a hand on her shoulder. "It's fine. I've got this."

The arch is made up of a series of boxes. Each box is two foot by two foot square, the same symbol carved into each box. I find a cop car nearby.

The vehicle is far enough away from the arch I can use magic to hotwire the ignition. I shift into gear and drive straight through the arch. Chunks of wood boxes dent the roof and crack the glass. I grab the vehicles shotgun as I exit. Most of the boxes are splinters from the impact, but I find a mostly solid piece.

The top and bottom of the box is empty of carvings. I set the box down and smash the top with the butt of the shotgun. It takes a couple blows, but I break through the top of the box. Thankfully, the inside is hollow.

I walk the box back to Bartholomew and Fox.

"Trade me?" I hand Fox the shotgun and take her blade.

"No, no." Bartholomew shakes his head, watching the box with wide eyes. He gasps for magic, but I soak it all up.

I crouch down next to the half with the head. "Sorry, Bart, but I can't have you showing up and starting shit."

Fox's razor sharp blade slices through the skin and tendon with ease. The spinal cord is tougher, but I hack my way through, Bartholomew begging and pleading the whole way. I pick up the head by his white hair and toss it in the box. Immediately his attempt to draw magic ceases. The runes cut him off from everything.

"What are you going to do with it?" Fox asks.

I wipe her knife across Bartholomew's pants and hand the blade back. "We'll have to figure it out later. There are bigger fish to fry." I tuck the box under my arm and head back for the mustang.

"Are you okay to drive?" I ask. "I might need a second after all that excitement."

Vampire Valley

Chapter 30

With a mage head in a box shoved in the trunk of the mustang, Fox drives us toward the Glow.

My head aches from using magic. It's a throbbing kind of pain I can feel behind my eyeballs. There's no way I can cast the cloaking spell again, but I'm praying the cops were planning to catch us at the border to Hair Nation. Hopefully, patrols in the city won't be as strict.

Fox reaches over and takes my hand. "You okay?"

"I will be."

"Damn well better," Fox says. "We've got some sharps that need murdered."

"Yes, ma'am," I say.

Downtown passes in a blur, buildings reduce to plain gray streaks. I squeeze my eyes closed and try to clear my head. Everything is out of focus, but I don't think I'm going blind again. It's the small victories. We've got the shotgun from the cop car, and I still have the magic revolver with three rounds left. There's no telling how much magic mojo I'm going to be able to access. I wish we had more firepower, but there's no going back now.

We make it through downtown without issue and into the Glow.

"So, where to?" Fox asks.

"Do you remember where we met?"

"That bar over on Keller Street?"

"No, the *first* time you met me."

Fox eyes me. "The Dame?"

"Yup."

The Dame is a bar on the south end of the Glow. It used to be a great jazz club back in the forties, but it went out of business in the seventies. Some asshole bought it in the nineties and tried to revive it. He kept the name and made it up to look like a cool retro club, but it was a shithole. The Glow is full of dives and the Dame might be the dive-iest of them all.

By the time Fox pulls up in front of The Dame, my head is almost back to normal. My vision is still blurry, but it's more an inconvenience than debilitating. Fox parks in a small lot across from the bar. It's still early. The bar doesn't open for a few more hours yet. A lone Ford Tempo takes up the same space it has for the last decade.

We get out of the car. I hold the shotgun out to Fox. She shakes her head and holds up her katana. I tuck the shotgun stock into my armpit and hold the gun by the pump, trying to conceal it inside my arm as I walk across the street.

The alley next to the bar smells like shit and garbage. Trash overflows a dumpster and carpets the ground. Used condoms float in puddles of piss like the bobbers of someone fishing for syphilis.

I hold a finger up to my lips as we creep in between the buildings. The window from my dreams is on the right side. None of the doors are labelled. A rickety fire escape leads up the side of the building, just beyond the window.

The air feels sick, a hair-of-the-dog misery hangs like a cloud. I taste bile as I draw in the magic. The back of my nostrils burn with someone else's puke.

Fox points at her eyes, and then at the window. I shake my head and point at the door. There's no point to look through the window and risk getting spotted. We go through the front door and see what the hell happens. This deep in the Glow, even if there aren't sharps holding a hair hostage behind door number one, it's probably not going to be some upstanding family eating a quiet dinner.

We take our places on either side of the door. I hold up my fingers in a silent countdown.

Three...

I use a touch of magic to unbolt the door.

Two...

The magic turns the handle and cracks the door open.

One...

I put my boot into the door. The door swings open and reveals a chair in the middle of the room. Jordon sits tied to the chair, bloody bandage wrapped around the hand with his missing finger.

Daylight shines in through the open door. Two sharps are pressed against the far wall, both pointing guns in our direction. I pump the shotgun and fire at the same time as the sharp in front of me. Searing pain burns through my chest as I watch the vampire crumple to the ground.

My lungs stutter in my chest. Something warm oozes down my left side. I look down at a small hole in my breast. Each pump of my heart sends more crimson pouring from the hole. Pressing my palm to the wound, I focus on the pain. My arhythmic heartbeat slows. Then stops. The edges of my vision fade to black for a moment before my heart jump starts back to life. Steady breaths, in and out. I pull my hand away to find the wound closed.

Still not sure if this is some new power from the deal with Sarah, but that's way better than rebirth.

The sharp who shot me is in a heap on the floor, a bloody mess where his face used to be. The other one is wrapped in the fetal position on the ground, blood gushes past the knife sticking out of his throat. I rush over to the living one and grab his collar.

"Who hired you?"

The pale, calm vampire stares at me for a second before his eyes roll back in his head.

"Fuck." I hold out my arm. "I'll give you permission to bite me if you tell me who hired you?"

It's no use. He's gone. Sharps don't have much blood on hand, and they bleed out faster than a standard.

"Useless bastard." I dig through his pockets, hoping to find anything remotely incriminating.

My hand lands on something. I slide a cheap, flip phone out. The call history shows a handful of back and forth calls with the same contact "D". It's the only contact in the phone.

I slide the phone into my pocket and get up to check the other body. Fox has cut Jordon free and is examining him for injuries.

The other sharp has even less to offer, no wallet, no keys, no phone, nothing. Whoever hired them must have dropped them off here with nothing but a captive hair and a burner phone.

"He okay?" I ask as I walk around the room.

"He will be."

Werewolves heal fast and Jordon is young. He should sprout a finger back pretty quick.

The rest of the room is standard issue kidnapper stuff. Small TV, couple chairs, minifridge stocked with beers round out the décor. A prepaid credit card sits under the TV. I slide the card into my pocket. The shit is impossible to trace back to an owner, but I'll never turn down some cash.

I toss the phone to Fox.

She clicks around on the keys. "D for Darius?"

"I guess."

The pieces feel like I'm squeezing them into place, that puzzle piece you swear was cut just a little wrong, so you jam it into place anyway. Darius is worried about a power challenge and needs a friend. Burgess is worried about Sarah and needs some muscle. The old man hires out the vampire to distract the hairs, keep them from getting in the way.

The theory makes sense if you tilt your head to the side when you look at it. I don't know that I like it, but Occam's Razor and all that. Nothing else makes any amount of sense.

"Come on, kid. Let's get you home."

Chapter 31

I'm not a fan of stuffing the six-foot something Jordon in the back seat of the mustang, but I don't like stealing cars from the Glow. No one down here has shit and taking from them just feels bad.

We pile into the car. "Where to?"

"We have to get Jordon home and then figure out our next move."

Jordon sits quietly in the back seat with his knees shoved up to his chin.

"You good, kid?" I snap my fingers in front of his face.

"Yeah. Yeah, I'm good." His voice is a little far out, but his eyes seem sharp.

"Did anyone say anything? Tell you who did this?"

"No, they didn't talk. Just sat around and watched Lions games."

"Shit," I say. "They held you captive *and* tortured you? Those monsters."

The kid either doesn't get the joke or doesn't find it funny. I start the car and pull out onto the road.

Fox's phone rings. She checks the screen, swipes her finger to end the call. Has to be her mom again. I want to help, to make her feel better. I want to save her the way she did me. *Hey, honey, do you want me to murder your mom for you?* That's what a good husband would do, right? Should I murder her and *not* ask Fox? Who knew dealing with in-laws would be so complicated?

Her phone rings again. "The fuck do you want?" Fox hovers her finger over the red 'end' button. "Oh." She answers the call on speaker. "Hey, Sarah. What's up?"

"I wanted to call you with an update," Sarah says. "Do you still suspect Darius in the disappearance of your young hair friend?"

Fox looks over at me. I give her a nod. It has to be Darius.

"We do," Fox says.

"I still have an in at the office. Lloyd's personal assistant owes me some favors and she keeps me informed of his schedule."

That's awful handy.

"He has a meeting at eight tonight with Darius."

That's a real two birds on a sliver platter kind of booking. Burgess and Darius have to die for their sins. Getting them both in the same place seems like the perfect time.

"Okay," Fox says.

After a pause, Sarah asks, "Are you going after them?"

"We have to talk about it," Fox says.

"If you do, be careful. I can't be seen there, can't be associated with anything that might happen."

"I get it," Fox snaps.

"But I mean it, be careful. If I can help in any other way, tell me. I want you to know I'm there for you, Fox."

"Got it. Thanks." Fox ends the call.

"What the hell do we do now?" Fox tosses the phone in her lap.

I shrug, drive toward Burgess tower. "Seems like now's as good a time as ever. I'm going to kill Burgess."

"And Darius has to pay for what he did to the pack," Jordon says from the back seat.

"Who asked you, kid?"

Fox punches my shoulder. "The kid's not wrong."

"I know. I know."

Afternoon traffic picks up. People are getting off work and heading for bars. A sedan with Roswell flags tucked in the windows drives by. The 'o' in Roswell is an alien head. I'll have to ask Sarah if Aliens are part of her Mountain City alliance.

A small pack of hairs walk down the sidewalk, a mini pack. The hairs tend to gravitate toward the main pack in Hair Nation, but some prefer the isolation of small groups. A guy in a flannel shirt pounds a fist against his chest and howls. His girlfriend's cheeks blush and she pushes away. Jordon shifts in his seat, knocking his knees into my back.

"Easy back there, killer," I say.

"It's not right," Jordon mumbles. "They should be with the pack."

"Do you know them?" I put my blinker on and turn on the main highway to downtown.

"No."

"What the hell does it matter then?"

Fox elbows me.

"Whatever. You don't get it."

The traffic leaving downtown is bumper to bumper. It's a wide open road on the way in. Cops don't appear to be out in any special show. Maybe they are trying to figure out what the fuck happened back at the check point. I should probably check on Bartholomew's head. Later.

There's a parking garage across from Burgess tower. This late in the evening, the gates are up and the guard has gone home. I circle up to the roof and park.

Jordon groans as he climbs out of the car and stretches his legs. I slam the door and stare at a hundred floors of Burgess excess.

Fox hops on the hood. "What are you thinking?"

"Vampire, probably more than one, at night. Plus, whatever security Burgess has." I lean against the front of the car and wrap my arms around Fox's waist. "If we go in now, it's going to be pretty heavy."

"You scared?" She nudges me with her elbow.

"Scared? I'm apparently more immortal now than ever before. I'm just not sure what kind of mess we're getting into."

"Burgess leans toward mages for security. Maybe we get lucky and the mages and sharps cancel each other out."

"I'll help." Jordon looks over the edge of the parking garage.

"Hell you will," Fox says. "You had your finger chopped off."

"But I—"

"But you'll nothing."

"You need backup."

"Maybe we do," she says.

"Wait, what?" That is not what I expected to hear.

Fox takes out her phone. She dials a number and turns on the speaker. "Hey, Ethan. We got Jordon back."

"Thank god," Ethan says. "Is everyone okay?"

"We're fine."

Actually, I got shot in the heart. I look down at my bloodstained shirt. Not exactly what I'd call fine.

"Where are you?"

"Well, fun story," Fox says. Her eyes twinkle with that look she gets when she's about to pull some shit. "We're across the street from Burgess Towers."

"What?" A moment of silence. Then Ethan's voice from further away, "Why are you at Burgess Towers?"

"We're pretty sure it was Darius who took Jordon. And we got a tip that Darius is meeting Burgess here in…" Fox checks the time on her phone. "Just under two hours."

A low growl through the phone speaker. Jordon's muscles flex and twitch under his shirt.

"What do you need?" Ethan's voice is harsh. He sounds like he's ready to march his ass down here right now.

"We need some backup."

"I'm here, Ethan," Jordon says.

Fox starts, "He—"

But Ethan carries over the top. "You are in no condition for anything right now. The only thing you will do is get your ass back to your mother so she can stop worrying about you."

Jordon pouts and kicks at the car tire.

"We need some backup," Fox says.

"I'll be righ—"

"Discrete backup," I say. "There's no guarantee this doesn't go sideways and the pack alpha getting caught trying to assassinate Burgess is bad business for everyone."

There's a tense silence. I can feel Ethan's fury. Ethan getting spotted within ten square miles of a Burgess murder would have O'Malley screaming from the twenty-four hour news cycle rooftops for the next two months.

"How many?" Ethan says.

Fox looks to me. I hold up four fingers. It's enough for a strike team, but small enough for plausible deniability. A dozen hairs points straight to Hair Nation. A few hairs, an immortal, and a kitsune could be just about anything. If we all die they'll probably call Fox and I standards anyway.

Fuckers.

"Four should be plenty," Fox says.

"You'll have four of my best. Where exactly should I send them?"

"We're on top of the McGinnley Parking Garage. I'm going to send Jordon home in our car, but Sam and I will be waiting."

Jordon grumbles and plays footsie with the car tire some more. I think the Mustang's taking a real shine to him.

"They'll be there."

"Thank you."

"Hey, Fox?"

"Yeah."

"Please be careful."

"Thanks, Ethan." She ends the call and puts the phone back in her pocket.

"You know," I say. "Sure would be nice if someone would tell me to be careful." I fake a sad face.

"Are you jealous?"

"Maybe?"

"Do you want me to tell you to be careful?"

"Maybe."

"Hey, Sam?"

"Yeah?"

"Cowboy the fuck up."

Vampire Valley

Chapter 32

Fox and I sit on the edge of the parking garage watching the traffic pass by below. Jordon left in a fit thirty minutes ago. The hair backup should be here soon. We've still got an hour or so before Burgess's meeting with Darius.

The building rumbles as a pack of angry motorcycles roar through the city below. We're too far up to make out their patches, but they have the same general look as the fuckers we stole our rides from yesterday.

"What do you think their deal is?" I ask.

Fox watches them pass below. "The Seeds of Adam?"

I'd forgotten their name. "Yeah. Those guys."

"Who knows? Just another biker gang."

A set of headlights turn into the parking garage below.

"That's probably our backup," Fox says.

"Probably."

We kept the police shotgun and I've still got the magic revolver. Fox has her orange katana and however many blades she has hidden on her person. I honestly feel under-prepared. Hopefully, the hairs bring some extra fire power.

An older black Jeep Cherokee parks and Elsa, Gabriel, Jaxon, and Anna pour out of the doors. All are dressed in black tactical gear.

Elsa gives us a nod and leads us to the back. She pops the hatch revealing a small armory.

"Hello, beautiful," Fox traces her finger across the receiver of a Mark 18 close quarters battle rifle. "Five oh five six?"

"Nah. Three hundred blackout." Gabriel passes her the gun.

Fox grins as she turns on a red sighting dot, aiming at phantom targets, testing the weight.

"That's a lot of gun for little girl," Anna spits in her hateful accent. She laughs and looks to Jaxon.

Jaxon silently shakes his head and reaches past Anna for a similar rifle.

Anna rolls her eyes. "What? You're on her side now?"

Jaxon takes his gun to the front of the Jeep to check the weapon and his pockets. Turns out kicking someone's ballsack off does a lot for inspiring allegiance. Or at least shut-the-fuck-up-ance.

I tuck another Glock into the back of my pants next to the magic revolver and grab the shotgun I jacked from the cop car earlier.

"What are you, the Terminator?" Gabriel takes the Mossberg out of my hand and passes me a gun that looks like something out of a sci-fi movie. "Tavor TS12. Three tube rotating magazine, five rounds per tube."

The gun feels foreign in my hands, but the thing looks like it could street sweep two city blocks. Who said all magic weapons have to be *actual* magic?

"Thanks."

"Hey, you all hear this?" Jaxon reaches through the open driver's door and turns up the radio.

A bored reporter says, "Sarah Roswell has called a press conference. She hasn't released any information about the subject matter. The conference will start in just under thirty minutes."

Fox laughs. "Convenient timing."

"Plausible deniability," I say. "Someone should call and see if they can get Ethan on there with her. Burgess turns up dead, eyes are gonna be on both of them."

"Ethan's still laid up after the sharp attack," Elsa says.

"And besides," Gabriel adds, "Everyone in the town knows Ethan is too smart to do the work himself. They'll either think it was him or they won't. It doesn't matter."

We finish our final checks. The longer I hold this shotgun, the more I want to pump fifteen slugs into something. This stupid thing is drowning out the magic pistol singing at my back.

"Everybody ready to go?" I ask.

Hair Team Six gathers round.

"Do you want comms?" Gabriel asks.

"What?" I ask.

Gabriel taps his earpiece. "Communication device?"

"Do I need it?"

"Keep you from getting your damn ears blown out when you go all berserker with that shotgun."

"It'll be fine. I said we needed backup. We're not invading a royal palace."

Anna stares across at the shining beacon that is Burgess towers. "Are you so sure about that?"

"Yes. Well, no." What a pain in my ass. "Just give me the damn earbuds."

Fox is already clipping a radio to her shirt.

"Good choice." Gabriel tosses me a radio and earpieces.

"Thanks. Are we ready now?"

Nods all around.

"Okay, I think I can put some cloaking hoodoo on us. It's late, so I don't expect much in the way of people inside. We get in, take the stairs to the top."

"And when we get to the top?" Anna says with a scowl.

"Kill anything that moves." Fox walks past me. She pauses. "Oh, hey. Someone tell Sam to be careful."

"What?" Gabriel asks.

"Just tell him."

"Be careful." Jaxon knocks into my shoulder as he pushes past to the parking garage exit.

Chapter 33

On the sidewalk across from the tower, I tap into the city's energy. Although most of the stooges have gone home, the energy in the air remains the same. Here, in the city, there's a whirlwind of magic. There's a sense of anonymity. So many people it's hard to single out just one. That's exactly the magic I need.

Focusing in on the idea of discretion, I cast a net of stealth around us. Hopefully, it's enough to fool the security cameras. A magic user will probably see through it, but I'm hoping all the mages will be on the top floor guarding Lloyd's rich ass and not in the lobby.

"Everyone, stay close."

I lead the team across the street.

The front door of the tower swings open. A sharp in a business suit walks out. He's got a long cloak-like garment draped over his arm. The vampire looks right through us as he smiles into the evening air and practically skips away from the tower.

The invisibility cloaking must be working. This magic shit makes stuff way easier. I should have sold my soul to the devil years ago.

I wave my hand for them to follow. We make it through the doors. A bored clerk sits behind a tall desk. He cocks his head at the door as it swings closed behind Elsa. The confused look last for a moment before he goes back to clicking on his phone.

A pair of elevators sit to the right. Down the hall is a door marked 'stairs.' I open the door as quiet as I can and we all sneak inside.

It's something like ten million stairs to the top level of the tower, but the elevator would lose all sense of surprise. Fox and I are both huffing and puffing by the time we get to the top level. All four hairs look cool as if we were on a stroll around the block, dicks. Let's see them rip open a parking lot and swallow a guy.

I hold my hand up for a break and catch my breath with hands on my knees. Once my heart rate falls back, I wipe sweat off my forehead.

"Alright, I'll go in first," I say. "You guys cover me."

Jaxon snorts. "The skinny guy with no armor goes in first?"

"How many times can you come back to life after getting shot in the head?"

Jaxon looks at the ground.

I think about how we do this. Do I go in first? Talk to Burgess? What the hell do we have to talk about? Just walk in and tell him I'm going to kill him? Seems like a bad plan. Fuck it. We go in and light these fuckers up and be done with it.

The door has a sliver of a window. I try to get a look at the hallway but can't see shit. If anyone is standing guard outside Burgess's office, they'll get tipped off as soon as the stairwell door opens on its own. It's do or die.

I press open the door and into a small hall. We walk down the hall and come to the reception area outside Burgess's office. The little desk that held the old man's Sarah-look-a-like assistant is empty now.

A guard stands on either side of the office door. They're both scanning the room, fingers on the triggers of assault rifles. This must be some fucking awesome cloaking spell.

I point to the guard on the right and Fox nods. I give three small nods. On third we both open fire. Fox squeezes off four rounds in quick succession, two to the chest, two to the head. The guard is dead before he can draw his weapon.

My target gets three slugs. His body falls, leaving a mist of blood hanging in the air where his head used to be. Brain matter splatters against a painting on the wall behind him like a fucked-up Pollack painting. I squint to look through the gore. Fuck me, it *was* a Pollack. The crimson bits might be an improvement over the original.

"Go, go, go." Elsa's voice is clear through my earbud.

It's a vast improvement over the ringing that would normally accompany firing off guns in tight spaces.

A vacuum of magic sweeps toward the double doors of Burgess's office. I wish I could tell how many mages are in there, but I don't have enough experience. The energy pulls in three distinct directions.

"There's at least three mages in there," I say.

Fox grabs one handle and I take the other. We swing open the doors in tandem. The four tactical hairs file in the room. Jaxon and Anna go left, Elsa and Gabriel right.

As soon as we enter, I feel my cloaking spell pulled away like a blanket ripped off our heads.

The room should contain Burgess, Darius, and appropriate amounts of security. Darius is nowhere in sight. A woman in a regal kimono sits in front of Burgess's desk.

"The fuck? Mom?" Fox says.

Looks like Fox was right about her mom feeding Burgess information. Ratting out your own daughter to convince her to go home is a real dick move.

Four mages stand along the glass walls, all have weapons trained in our directions. Two samurai stand at Hisa's back.

I freeze. Do I give a command to start shooting with Fox's mom here? Hell, I was thinking about killing her myself not long ago.

Fox does not suffer from my indecision. She pops off another four rounds at the samurai closest. The sound is like a firing pistol signaling the start of a cluster fuck.

All four hairs open up on the mages. Energy whishes past me as one of them puts up a shield to block the bullets. The two samurai draw swords and come at me.

Shit.

I squeeze off two rounds, rotate the ammo tube, and then fire another five. The slugs bounce off the samurai's magically charged armor.

One of the hairs yells something in my ear. I don't catch the words.

"This didn't work out so well for your friends," I say.

The threat doesn't seem to carry any weight. I toss the shotgun to the side and draw on the energy in the room. Between the four mages and samurai bodyguards, I have to fight over the magic. It's like a seven-way tug of war over a saltwater taffy, if the taffy were plastic explosives and the seven people were all blast caps.

I try to get a bead on the magic. It tastes like licking a twenty-dollar bill. There's a madness attached to it, the kind of greed that could buy up all the oxygen in the world just to say they owned it. The insatiability I can work with. I use the greedy energy to work a spell that draws more energy.

"Shields are down," Elsa says.

Gunfire pops off at a steady rate around me.

"Somethings wrong," Anna says in my ear. "I can't move."

Something snarls in my ear. A gray wolf tears across the room.

Burgess's office is comically covered in gold fixtures. Gold isn't the strongest metal, but it's stronger than flesh. I focus the greedy energy on the metal. A katana slices at my throat, but my now solid skin stops the blade in its tracks. I grab the blade with my left hand and twist pulling the samurai off balance. As he stumbles, I reach my right arm behind me for the Glock. I plant the barrel under his chin and squeeze the trigger.

The bullet passes through his head, bottom to top, and knocks his metal helmet to the ground.

A wave of pressure hits me from the side. The feeling is like being inside a speaker the size of Texas with the bass turned up to eleven. The impact knocks me over a small display cabinet of gold bullshit. I hit the ground and roll, trying to find my way up to my feet. My chest aches.

From the corner of my vision, I watch a brown wolf pounce on a mage. The gunfire has slowed now, just an occasional shot. To my left, Burgess closes himself behind a solid steel door. The thing looks like a bank vault. With his kind of money, a panic room makes sense.

Another wave of energy heads for the samurai who just levelled my ass. I focus on him, on stealing the magic away. He plants his feet and his forehead crumples as we play tug of war. It takes an effort, but the meter turns in my favor. I focus on drawing more while also trying to spin an attack spell.

The overabundance and lavishness of the office gives me an idea. I let go of the magical rope. The energy rushes at the samurai. I use what I have to turn on the jets and shove it down his throat. The man's eyes go wide as his stomach swells.

His hands claw across his stomach as he tries to force me to stop. Fox's hand grabs the top of his helmet from behind. She pulls his head back and slits his throat. Blood burbles from the wound.

I scan the room. All the mages are dead, one took a bullet between the eyes, two have been mauled by werewolves, and one is just a headless body. Fox's work, no doubt. Fully naked, Gabriel and Elsa stand in front of Anna. Her eyes flit back and forth, but she's frozen in place.

A black wolf lopes across the room, turning into Jaxon mid-stride. He snaps his fingers in front of Anna's face a few times. "Can you help her?" he says to me.

"Can she stop being a dick to me?"

Jaxon growls.

"What?" I ask. "It's a fair question."

"Sam." Elsa says my name in that tone of parental disappointment.

I sigh in that tone of teenage defeat. "Fine."

With all the other mages dead, it's easy to top off the tanks. The spell the mage cast on Anna is sloppy. I would have expected more out of someone on Burgess's payroll. I guess spellcasting is harder when there are wolves beating down your door. The spell is a living thing, hovering around Anna. Tendrils of magic snake around her body and root into the granite flooring of the office.

One of the vines glows brighter than the others. I focus on that one, pulling at it with my mind. The thing comes apart smoother than silk.

Anna drops to one knee, her chest heaves as she catches her breath. Once she levels out, she uses her rifle to push back to her feet. She crosses the room to one of the dead mages, fires a dozen shots into his head.

"Better?" Jaxon asks when she turns back around.

"Da." She swaps a fresh magazine.

I wonder if she's going to fire more shots but seems satisfied with the mage's deader than hell status. With that settled, I turn to the large panic room door.

"Do we have anything to deal with that?" I ask.

Gabriel laughs. "You're the magic man."

The door of the room resembles a bank vault, but with smooth steel on the outside. There's no handle, no combination dial, just a sheer wall of cute-try-but-fuck-you-very-much. A frame of runes is etched around the outside. For a guy who uses all mage security, Burgess sure is big on anti-magic devices.

I focus some energy on the door, try to open it from the inside, but there's just a wall of nothing. "Magic isn't going to do shit for this one. You guys have any explosives?"

Elsa sets her palm against the door. "It would take a dump truck worth of plastics to crack this thing."

Fox walks behind me and takes the magic revolver out of my waistband.

"Wait," I say.

"Wait what?" Fox levels the gun at the center of the door.

"There's only three bullets left."

"Do you want Burgess dead?"

"Yes."

Fox fires a round at the door. The gun sounds like a canon, through the ear protection. The whole room hums with a shockwave. Whatever kind of magic the sharps carved into that door, it is not prepared for the magic of the gun. Maybe the gun is magic and the bullet isn't. Maybe it's a kind of magic the sharps had never seen before, but whatever the reason the bullet blows a crater-sized hole through the vault.

I bend to peer through the door. Burgess is in a recliner, holding a cigar and a glass of amber liquor. A TV in front of him flashes images of Sarah's press conference. A giant circle of gore paints the far wall in blood. A pair of legs, clad in sheer stockings stand upright a foot in front of Burgess. The old man stares gape-jawed at the carnage. Smoke rises from the where thighs used to connect to a body.

Chapter 34

Burgess takes one last look at the wreckage of his in-panic-room stewardess and sits back in his recliner. He takes a drag off his cigar, chases it down with a drink. Sarah's on TV, in front of a podium. Burgess chuckles and it turns into a wet, hacking cough.

The old man nods at Sarah on the screen. "Plausible—"

The Glock isn't a bazooka like the magic pistol, but a half ounce of lead does the job all the same. Burgess's head snaps to the side. Blood splatters against the wall, a thumbnail portrait next to the mural that used to be his assistant.

Fox wraps her arm around me. We stare at the abattoir in silence.

"Mission complete," Elsa says. "We've got to go before cops show up. That was a lot of noise."

Fox kisses me on the cheek, puts the revolver back. "Time to go," she whispers.

I take one last look at the remains of the son of a bitch who killed my parents. The empty hole in my heart is still there. The guilt, the anger, the hate, none of the emotions have changed. The only difference in my life is Burgess is dead. Fox is safe. Safe from Burgess anyway.

Shit.

"Where is Fox's mom?"

We search the mess of an office. Four mages, two samurai, and no one else.

"Where the hell did she go?" Elsa asks.

"She has more magic than anyone else in this room," Fox says. "Except for Sam, maybe. It wouldn't have been hard for her to make an exit."

"Are you magic?" Gabriel asks.

"Fuckin' right I am." Fox winks at him. "Ow, fuck." Fox slaps her neck.

"Are you okay?" I rush to her side, unsure of what's going on or how to fix it.

"Yeah. I just…I don't know. Felt like something stung my neck." Fox pulls her hand away, revealing something truly magical.

"Ummmm…Fox?"

"What? What is it?"

"Sune." I point at the fox tattoo on her neck.

"Huh?" Fox holds her arm out.

The tattoo crawls from Fox's neck down her shoulder and onto her forearm. The tattoo looks over its shoulder and notices a second tail. The fox grins. It struts up and down Fox's arm, sashaying its tail side to side with each step.

"That's new," Fox says. "Told you I was magic." She grins at Gabriel.

And here I thought her never-ending supply of blades was magic.

"Do you feel…different?" I ask.

Fox flexes her hands open and closed, rolls her head around. "You know, honestly, I do. I feel pretty fucking great."

"Good job," Anna barks. "You get new tail. Can we go now?"

Fox glares at Anna but takes a step toward the exit anyway. With that kind of attitude, the hair's going to need a swift kick in the balls as well.

"You know who else is missing?" Elsa says.

"Darius," Fox and I say together.

"What's that about?" Elsa scans the room one last time.

"Maybe he got cold feet," Fox says.

"Maybe." I climb through the gap in the safe room door.

A trail of smoke rises from Burgess's cigar. The old man still has the glass of scotch grasped in his greedy mitt.

"What are you doing?" Fox says from the office.

I wave a hand and dig through the old man's pockets.

"Are you seriously looting a corpse?" Gabriel throws his hands up.

I find his cell phone in an inner pocket. There's no time to look through it now, but it might provide some answers. I pocket the phone and climb back into the office.

"Let's get out of here," I say.

We walk back to the hallway.

"Stairs again?" Elsa reaches for the door to the stairwell.

"There's no one left to surprise." I gather magic to cast a cloaking spell again. "Let's take the elevator." I press the call button.

"Hey," Jaxon nudges my elbow and points at the floor marker above the doors.

The elevator car is already at floor ten and climbing. This late at night, there shouldn't be anyone else in the building.

"Fan out. Take cover."

We split up on either side of the hall. Red dots from laser sights scan across the polished metal doors. The revolver sings to me again. Shut up, gun. You've already had your fun tonight. I rotate the tube of the shotgun, giving me access to five more rounds.

The laser sights steady at chest level as the elevator reaches the top floor. With a gentle 'bing,' the doors slide open to reveal Darius and two guards.

Darius has his head tilted back, laughing. A long white robe hangs over his body. It's full dark outside and he's not wearing any head covering. For a thousands-year old man, Darius looks like a twenty something out for a night on the town. His bright white teeth shine in the well-lit elevator compartment.

His two guards reach for their weapons.

The six of us unload into the elevator car. Vampires are fast at night, faster than anything I've seen. No amount of speed can make up for the surprise attack though. The men are cornered in the small space, nowhere to go.

The elevator chimes. The doors attempt to slide closed, ram a dead body, open again.

Elsa puts two fingers at her temple, nods, points, and does something else that I don't catch. I'm pretty sure she wants me to throw a fastball high and inside.

"Fuck this." Fox drops her gun and marches toward the elevator.

I follow behind while the hairs reload.

Black ichor covers the inside of the car. One sharp is collapsed across the floor. The elevator chimes and tries to close again with the same result. The other sharp guard is in the corner, his corpse an unrecognizable mess of bullet holes.

"Where the fuck is—" I start.

A pair of sandaled feet swing down from the top of the elevator car, slamming into my chest. The impact breaks ribs. Splintered bone digs into organs with every breath. Fuck. Not now. Come on.

I struggle to find my footing but can't. The hairs have their weapons trained on the elevator, but Fox is too close. Hand to hand combat with a sharp is bad news. They are fast. Fox is fast too, but I don't think I've ever seen anything move as quick as a vampire on the attack.

All I can do is lay and watch and pray my body stitches itself together in time to help.

Darius grabs at Fox, but he's…he's too slow. She ducks his grip. Faster than I've ever seen her move, she's suddenly behind him. Seven inches of glowing orange energy forms in her palm. It looks like a light saber version of an ice pick. Fox jams the weapon into Darius neck a dozen times before the vampire even realizes she's behind him. Black blood oozes out the side of his throat.

Sharps can come back from a lot, all they need is a drop of blood from the living. There's one way to be sure. Fox's energy ice pick warps from a sharp point to a flat blade, she draws the weapon across Darius's throat. The blade cuts through flesh and bone like butter. Fox decapitates the other two sharps, leaving all three bodies in the elevator

I groan as my ribs choose right now to snap back into place. Thanks, body. I push myself back to my feet. "So," I say, "About those stairs."

Anna grunts as she pushes open the stairwell door. I cast the cloaking spell over all of us as we start our trek to the lobby.

Halfway down, Elsa says, "Anyone else think it's weird Darius was late for his meeting with Burgess?"

"Yes, it is," I say.

"They want to measure cock," Anna says. "He shows up late, establishes dominance."

None of us have any better suggestions.

Once we cross the street, I drop the cloak. A wave of nausea passes over me. My legs shake, but I catch myself. Fox holds my elbow and steadies me.

"You good?"

"I will be."

We get to the Jeep on the roof and all stare at the five-seater in contemplation. The trunk is stocked full of guns.

"Ummm…" Gabriel trails off.

"It's fine," I say. "There was a Volvo down on the bottom level."

"You sure?"

"Sure."

Fox and I head down for the safety-box. There's no one in the garage at this hour and it's easy enough to pop the locks and start the engine.

"You care to drive?" I ask.

Fox opens the door. "You okay?"

"Just done a little bit of heavy lifting today and don't want to pass out on a hairpin curve."

"Okay then."

Sitting in the fuzzy car seat feels like ecstasy. A day's worth of using magic I didn't have a week ago punches me square between the eyes. It hurts worse than the sharp shooting me. I close my eyes and rest my head against the door.

A bump in the road smacks my face against the window glass. I open my eyes and check the streets. We're halfway to Hair Nation. Fox has her hands resting on the bottom of the steering wheel, gently driving us up the hill. A smile plays on the edges of her lips. Spatters of blood cover her cheek.

I reach across and cup her cheek in my hand. She hums and nuzzles against my palm.

"Hey there," she says.

"Hey there."

"I thought you were dead."

"Maybe next time."

"So, you have two tails now."

"Apparently."

"Did you know that could happen?"

Fox shrugs. "I knew it could. Mother always said tails come with experience and they are a form of power."

I think back on Fox's mom. Her fox had a lot of tails. "What do you think made you sprout one now?"

Fox thinks for a few curves. "Hisa always said that I had to study in the ways of the kitsune for Sune to grow more tails. It's part of why she didn't want me to leave. She insisted I spend my life in the library reading, to grow my power."

"Uh-huh. Have you been doing a lot of reading between gun fights?"

"Not so much, but now that I think about it, Hisa didn't say knowledge, she said experience. My only real power, has been my ability to summon blades."

Ha! It *is* magic.

"Maybe it was experience in combat," Fox says. "It was the after the fight with Lloyd's bodyguards. Maybe I, fuck, levelled up or something?"

"You moved faster than a demon and summoned a glowing blade out of your hand," I say.

Fox smiles ear to ear. "Yeah. I did. It was great. I've never wielded a blade that sharp. It was amazing."

My pocket buzzes. Oh, shit. Bartholomew. I left his head in the trunk of the mustang. Hopefully, Jordon didn't check the car out too close when he took it home. Anyway, Bartholomew was the prank caller and he doesn't have fingers anymore. Who the fuck is calling me?

I grab the buzzing device, trying to figure out why it feels weird in my hand. The bright light of Burgess's phone assaults my eyes. Someone named "Sasha" is calling. I end the call.

"Is that the old man's phone?" Fox glances over.

"Yeah."

"Why did you take it?"

"Dunno."

I flip through the text messages. Lots of shit about meetings and business and corporate circle-jerking. Great to see you on the links yesterday, Lloyd. Jolly good match. Glad you took it home with my driving iron. Some shit like that. Texts are a dead end so I switch to email.

The interior of the car feels like a furnace. The a/c is on, but it's blowing half-assed version of cool at my belly button. I try to turn the vent at my face and the plastic tab breaks off. Fox snorts. Even Sune is parked on Fox's neck silently huffing at me.

Sneaky ass tattoo.

Dropping the broken vent, I use the hand crank to roll my window down. Warm air blows on my face, but at least it's not suffocating, not yet. Summer's on its way.

I flip through Lloyd's emails. They are mostly billing receipts and calendar invites. I strike paydirt in the deleted folder.

"Huh," I say.

"Huh what?"

"It's an email from Darius's people, confirming his appointment at eight-thirty."

Fox tilts her head. "I thought Sarah said eight."

"She did."

"So why tell us eight-thirty?"

I roll it over in my head a bit. "Could be a case of telephone. She heard it from someone who heard it from someone else."

"She knew we were going to assassinate Burgess. Giving us the right time seems like a pretty big fucking deal."

I flip the phone in circles in my hand, trying to work out an answer. "What if she wanted to be sure we got Burgess? Maybe she wasn't sure if we could take them all if the sharps were there?"

"That doesn't sound right."

"It's the best I've got for now."

Fox bites her lip but relaxes back into her seat.

Bone tired weariness sets back in. I grab the release to lean my seat back and it breaks off. "Fuck this fucking piece of shit car."

Chapter 35

"Hey, wake up," Fox says. "You're going to want to see this."

Where the fuck am I and how did I get here?

Every cell of my body hurts. My hair hurts. How does goddamn hair hurt? Really. How is that possible?

I sit up in bed. Ethan's bed. Looks like we made it back to Hair Nation alright.

Ethan is standing in front of the television. He's wearing a suit that's perfectly tailored to his football linebacker physique.

"Looks—" My voice catches in my throat. I cough and try again. "Looks like you're feeling better."

Ethan grins at me. No, no it's not a wolfish grin. Don't even put that shit on me.

"Much."

"Shhh. Look." Fox points at the screen.

A non-O'Malley newscaster babbles on about something. Has the volume been on this whole time? I focus on the TV. The forty-something news guy in his cheap suit and over-sprayed hair speaks directly into the camera.

"...mogul Lloyd Burgess dead in his office. Sources with MCPD are saying the murder came as a result of a contract dispute."

Ethan clicks off the volume. "They are saying Darius and Burgess blew up. Burgess was hiring up sharps and they are saying it was a dispute over wages."

Sarah's timing makes some amount of sense. "She put us all up there together so this could happen," I say.

"I bet she already had people spinning this story up before we ever stepped foot in Burgess Tower." Fox scoffs.

Ethan plops down into a papasan chair. "The news isn't blaming it on my people, or even Sarah for that matter. I'll take this as a win."

"You getting into bed with her?" I ask.

Ethan growls.

"Not literally, of course."

The wolf eyes me. A week ago, I'd have crumpled up like last month's newspaper, but now? Fuck this guy. I give him the stink eye right back.

He laughs. "You're...different."

"Got killed enough to stop being afraid, of anything." Did that sound tough? I think it sounded tough.

"Good. I've come to terms with my Orange Coat leaving me for another man, but I couldn't accept her leaving me for a bitch. It's good to see you finally lifting your leg to piss."

"Hey, turn it up." Fox points at the screen again. "Who's that?"

The screen splits, the same guy on the left and a well-dressed sharp on the right. She's wearing a nice suit, black hair tied up in a bun. Burn scars of runes creep up the sides of her neck. A caption at the bottom of the screen reads: Burgess estate lawyer.

"You're telling me that Sarah Roswell was added back to Mr. Burgess's will?" the anchor asks, incredulity dripping from every word.

The sharp smiles. The gesture is practiced, showing enough teeth to convey emotion without the tips of her fangs peeking. "She was never removed."

"Never removed?" The guy can barely maintain a straight face. "After all the havoc she's caused for him, she was never removed?"

"That is correct."

"How? How is that possible?"

Another tempered smile. "Mr. Burgess was a wise man. He knew that young people, such as Ms. Roswell, are prone to fits of rebellion. He assumed it was a phase that would pass. My client thought there was no reason to remove his daughter from her birthright."

"Oh, hell no," I say.

Something isn't right. I turn Burgess's cell back on. There was something in his emails last night while I was snooping.

"What is that?" Ethan asks.

I ignore him, flipping through messages.

"Sam stole the old man's phone."

"Shit." Ethan stands out of his chair. "We've gotta get rid of that. Now." Ethan barks his command.

"Just a second." I hold a finger up. "Here."

I turn the phone around. In the sent folder, there's a very colorfully worded email to Hannah Levine Esquire demanding Roswell be cut from his will.

"Wait," Ethan says.

"This was dated a week ago." Fox takes the phone to look closer.

Ethan takes the phone from her hand, delicately. He turns the power off, snaps the thing in half. "We cannot have them track this here."

"…no other living relatives to contest the will," Hannah Levine Esquire says. "The will bequeaths all of Mr. Burgess's belongings to his sole heir, Sarah Burgess."

Ethan clicks off the TV.

Fox smiles. "I don't know how she did it, but you've got to give it to her. That broad is sneaky as all hell."

"The last time she was sneaky she killed my ass. Repeatedly."

Fox slinks across the room to me. She traces her finger across my neck. "But now you're all powerful and that's kinda hot."

Ethan's growl shakes the room.

The hair might scare me less now, but let's not push our luck. I slide away from Fox and off the other side of the bed. "What do we do now?"

"Our apartment is possibly still haunted."

"There is a bag of cash in our trunk."

"I love it when you talk dirty."

Ethan tosses the pieces of phone on the bed. He walks down the stairs from his loft without another word.

"Maybe he doesn't like ghosts," I say.

Fox laughs. Her phone chirps from across the room.

"Really. What now?" I ask.

She unplugs it from the charger and answers.

"Hello?"

"Can we meet?" Sarah says over the speaker.

"Why?" Fox is stoic.

"It'd mean a lot to me if we could speak in person."

"It might be a problem with the city's police force out to arrest us for that…misunderstanding the other day."

"It's taken care of," Sarah says.

Fox and I exchange a glance.

"Taken care of how?" Fox asks.

"Like you said, it was a misunderstanding. I spoke to the chief of police first thing this morning and cleared it up."

"That's…a thing you can do?"

I can hear Sarah smile over the phone. "It's amazing what you can accomplish with the right connections. Would you be able to be at the tower in an hour?"

Fox looks at our disheveled, blood-stained clothing. "Give us two."

"Very well. I'll let Percival know to expect you."

Chapter 36

Percival, a young sharp with a bright smile and no showing scars, greets us from the behind the main desk at the lobby.

"Mr. and Mrs. Flint," Percival says, "Welcome. Ms. Roswell is expecting you."

People in fancy suits move around the lobby. It's all cell phones pressed to faces and corporate power walks. No one shows a single sign the proprietor of this building was gunned down in his safe room last night.

The only difference between today and the last time I was here is the human to not-human ratio. A pair of sharp businessmen stop by the front doors to put on their Louis Vuitton head wraps. A troll passes by us and walks into the stairwell.

"Her office is on the second floor. Go on up," Percival says.

I take a step, stop. "Did you say the *second* floor?"

"Yes, sir."

Huh. The penthouse is clearly fucked, but I figured big shot Sarah would have at least taken the second from the top.

Fox and I ride the elevator up one floor.

The doors slide open to reveal a war room of sorts. A short hall leads to a wide-open conference room. Fox and I walk into a flurry of activity. A thousand-foot-long ancient oak table stretches from one end of the room to the other. Two dozen people are huddled in groups, shuffling through papers, and clacking away on laptops like their lives depend on it. I spot standards, sharps, two trolls in the far corner, and one guy with spiked hair who could be a stone or just a douche.

An almost familiar woman stands at the head of the table. She has the pale skin and black hair of Sarah, but her face is aged, lines showing at the corners of her eyes. The woman looks more like Sarah's mother, than Sarah.

The woman looks up from a pile of papers to see Fox and I. She beams a smile at my wife.

"Fox," she says. "Sam, come with me. Please."

She leads us to a small room off the left side of the conference room. The room is a kitchenette and break room. Microwave, single shot coffee machine, fridge, just the usual junk.

"Sarah?" Fox reaches her hand toward the woman's face but pulls it away without touching her.

"Yes," is all she says. Sarah grabs a few paper coffee cups and pods. She starts one cup brewing. The machine hisses and steams as a heavenly smelling stream of coffee fills the cup.

"Shut the door please."

I'm closest, so I close the door behind me. I hesitate with my hand over the lock button. Is this a closed door meeting or a locked door meeting? We assassinated her husband something like fourteen hours ago. Locked door seems like the safe answer. I click the button.

Sarah hands Fox a cup of coffee and starts a second. Fox grabs a few creamers and pours them in her cup.

"So," I say, "are we going to talk about this new look or are we supposed to just be cool with you adding on twenty-five years overnight?"

"The face of a young woman served its purpose, but now it's time to lead this city and no one wants to be led by a child."

"Right," I say.

Sarah lets it hang in the air a moment before she says, "Do you know Lloyd and I had only been married 10 years when I got sick?"

"No," I say. Never much cared for the lifestyles of the rich and the famous.

Fox sips her coffee, watches Sarah.

"By that time, I knew Lloyd had married me for my parent's money. Our marriage was a loveless, dead thing."

"You slept in separate bedrooms," I say. "So what?"

"Did it ever seem odd to you, the lengths Lloyd went to save the life of his wife, a woman he only married for money?"

Well, it hadn't until she said it like that. "A little bit," I say, trying to save some face as a P.I.

"Burgess Inc was successful, but it was far from an empire," Sarah says. "Lloyd needed steady investments from my father to keep his own business growing."

"And the investments would have ended if you died?" Fox asks.

"I was always honest with my mother, about my relationship with Lloyd. Everything I told her she told my father. My parents were old school romantics, met in high school when neither had a penny. They came up together, shared everything with each other." Sarah looks down at her hands.

"It was beautiful," Sarah says. "It's a kind of love you don't see much anymore." Sarah looks from Fox to me and back again with something close to sadness in her eyes.

Fox flinches like she wants to reach out to Sarah but doesn't quite know how to.

Sarah shrugs. "Anyway, father was pretty upset with the way Lloyd treated me. After I got sick, we made it very clear that my inheritance would be donated to charity."

"Bet Ol' Lloyd loved that," I say.

"It inspired him to find a cure for an uncurable disease. He ended up on Bartholomew and…well, your parents. By that point, I was so eat up with the sickness, I didn't know what was going on."

I'm still not sure what this has to do with Sarah looking older now, but I'm never one to interrupt a good story.

"When Bartholomew started his magic, I felt my soul leave my body, and it started stitching itself a new one."

"A feeling I know well."

Sarah nods. "I already felt the energy from the spell. Magic wasn't something I'd studied, but the amount of power Bartholomew worked into the spell, it was incredible. I'm not sure why, but I decided to make my body a young girl, instead of rebuilding my adult body again."

"Is that something you can do?" Fox asks, I'm not sure if she's talking to me or Sarah.

"Ummmmm, no," I say.

"I wasn't sure how I did it at the time, but my body ended up as a young child. When Lloyd asked what happened, I told him I didn't know."

"So why a kid's body?" I ask.

Sarah shoots me a narrow-eyed glare, like I just don't get it. "Because if I was a child, he couldn't touch me, couldn't expect me to continue acting as his wife. Especially, after he introduced me to everyone as his daughter. Using magic, I let myself age little at a time, but stopped in my teens. Lloyd was a private man, so the media never really paid attention to him having a teenage daughter for forty years, but they would have if word ever got out that he was trying to have a relationship with her. He rotated staff at the house, kept me a secret. It was fine, it gave me time to build."

"Oh," is the best I have for a comeback.

"I kept the façade up because Lloyd wanted to pretend this was about his inheritance and that played out better in the media for me anyway. At our interview, though, the whole city watched me use ghosts to catch that falling rafter. After seeing something like that, I don't think me appearing as a woman instead of a child will cause much concern."

"Cool," I say. "So, why are we on this floor?"

"The conference room is for meetings so far below Lloyd he couldn't be bothered." Sarah hands me a cup of coffee, starts on a third. "It's going to be my new operating space. There's another small room on the other side, I'm having it renovated to be my permanent office."

I take a sip of coffee. It's the best thing I've tasted in recent memory. "Situating yourself around the small people?"

Sarah smiles at me over her drink. "Something like that."

"Why did you call us here?" Fox rolls the edge of her cup around the small table.

"Ahhh, yes." Sarah sits opposite Fox. "I want to offer you a position with the organization."

Fox cracks up, almost knocks her half-full coffee off the table. She catches a glimpse of Sarah's face and stops cold. "Wait. You're serious?"

"Yes. Dead serious."

"Huh." Fox's gaze meets mine.

I don't even know what kind of response she's looking for. Seventy-two hours ago, we were leaving town. Now a job offer from the richest person in the city. There is not enough time or space in this room to even contemplate that kind of offer.

"And you as well, Sam," Sarah says.

"Right, but mostly her."

"I assumed you were a package deal."

"We are," Fox says. "Why? Why me?"

"I respect you. You are powerful. You know who you are and what you want. Honestly, you're a badass and this city needs more women like you. Women like us. Running this thing."

"Huh." Fox throws back the last of her coffee. "What's the job?"

"Community outreach to begin. You two both have connections in the Glow. I want to bring prosperity to the Glow and could use your help."

"That's a good one," I say. "The Glow is a dumpster fire. A cesspool of humanity circling down the drain of this city."

I expect a flare of anger, but nothing.

Sarah says, "You're right. It is now because Lloyd let it happen. Sam, you of all people should remember what it was like."

"The Glow was always shitty," I snap back.

"No. The Glow was always poor. It wasn't always a hot bed for drugs and violence. There's no reason it can't go back."

"Right," I say.

Sarah ignores me, keeps her eyes on Fox. "What do you say? We could make an unstoppable team." Now she looks back to bat her eyes at me. "The three of us."

"Ummm." Fox crumples her paper cup. "Can we think about it?"

"Of course. Here." Sarah reaches into her pocket and hands over a key fob. "Take my car, go back up to my chateau and think it over."

"Your chateau?" Fox raises an eyebrow.

"It's not as fancy as you might imagine, not too different from Sam's rebirth home. It was the first home my parents bought together. I've kept it renovated in their memory."

"What about you?"

Sarah blows a raspberry with her lips. "Did you see it out here? Between Lloyd's estate and meetings and fixing all that's been wrong with this city for the last fifty years, it'll be a blessing if I can get away from this building for five minutes in the next month."

I drink the last of my coffee, hoping to hide any expressions on my face. Sarah's offer is for Fox. Sure, she may have said both our names, but it's really for Fox. My wife has stuck with me through countless shitty P.I. jobs. If she wants to take one of her own, I've got her back.

"Ummmm…how do we get there?"

"Just get in my car and press home on the GPS. It will lead you there. The gate is synced to the car, it will open on its own."

Fox twirls the keys around her finger. "You up for a night in a chateau to talk over a job offer?"

Anything, literally anything is better than sleeping at my wife's ex-boyfriend's place. "Sure."

Sarah claps her hands. "Perfect. I'll have Annette bring the car around front." She takes Fox's hands in hers.

Fox cringes, but Sarah holds her grip tight. "You won't regret this. You'll see. I'm not Lloyd. I'm going to make everything better."

#####

As promised, a sleek German car is waiting for us at the front door. I take the driver's side this time. Fox punches around on the screen until the GPS lights up our path to Sarah's house. The map shows a location far north of the city.

She wasn't kidding, it really isn't far from the house where I was born. The place is beyond downtown and Hair Nation. It's up in the mountains. A place of solitude. That's good. After the last week, Fox and I could use some privacy.

"You think she has a hot tub?" I ease out into traffic, heading north.

"You think she's serious?"

"About which part?"

Fox rolls her window down, changes her mind and rolls it back up. "All of it. The job. Me?"

"I don't think she was lying."

"What does that mean?"

"It means, I think she meant everything she said. Zealots often are."

"You think she's crazy."

"I think she conned the hell out of me to join souls with her. And she sure set Burgess and Darius up without a sweat."

Fox slinks down in her chair. She traces her fingers along the wood grain.

"I'm not saying she's wrong or evil, just that she will do whatever it takes to get her way."

Fox doesn't say anything.

"Listen," I say. "Mountain City is full of injustices. Lloyd's war with the hairs chief among them. I believe that Sarah wants to change things and I believe that she thinks you can help her do that."

Fox rolls the window down again. She slides her shoes off and sticks her bare feet out the window. Her body angles as she leans against my shoulder. "Really?"

"Yes. You are a badass. Only an idiot wouldn't see that and Sarah Roswell is anything but an idiot."

"Awwww." She twists and kisses my neck. Her toes wave goodbye to the city as we pass onto the mountain road up to Sarah's cabin.

We drive in silence for miles. Fox is still enough to be asleep, but I know she's savoring the moment. Five minutes out from the chateau, I say, "Are you going to take the job?"

"You think I should?"

"I think you should if you want to."

"Do you think we can change things? Really change them?"

"I do," I say, leaving out the 'for better or worse' running through my mind. It's too soon to know if Sarah's Mountain City will be improved, or just different.

"You really don't mind staying here?"

"As long as I'm by your side, I'll be happy anywhere."

"Mean it?"

"Of course. Sand is over-rated anyway, gets all over the damn place."

"I think I'm going to do it."

"Let's do it then."

We pull up a mile long driveway to an iron fence with an intricate "R" worked into the middle. Silent motors sweep the gate inward, as Chateau De Roswell welcomes us into the life of Sarah Roswell.

The End

Thank you, so much for making it to the end of this novel. I hope it was a wild ride and everything you wanted it to be. Whether you loved it, hated it, or fall somewhere in between it would mean the world to me if you could throw a couple stars my way and maybe drop a word or two in a review. Reviews are the whiskey in the cup, well that and actual whiskey, that keep this writer writing.

While you wait on book 3, The Glow, to drop feel free to check out my other series: Beasts of Burdin

I know I already said this at the start of the book, but maybe you missed it there or you just forgot; I wouldn't blame you, I wrote it and I've already forgotten. Either way, it would make my day to talk to you about stories, this story, the funny story about the lady at the corner market who always shops with a goose in her buggy, whatever. Here are all the places you can reach me, don't hesitate to give me a shout.

Twitter: @AlexNaderWrites

Facebook: Facebook.com/alexnaderwrites

Instagram: @AlexNaderWrites

Website: https://alexnaderwrites.wixsite.com/my-site

Email: AlexNaderWrites@gmail.com

As a special thank you, anyone who signs up for the newsletter on my website will get a free ebook of Beasts of Burdin (The landing page says Necrotown, but since I'm guessing you've already read that I'll make sure you get a copy of Burdin). I promise to never email you more than once monthly and will do my best to only include cool shit.

Acknowledgements

I am always shit at this part. There are way to many people to thank and I always feel like a dick for forgetting someone. Thanks to Parker, Ryan, and Chris. You guys all listened to me bounce random ass ideas around while trying to figure out this book. Seth and Kay, thank you for all you input on the beta read. And Pam, thank you for a whole list of shit ranging from designing this book cover, to editing my braindead musings, to putting up with my bullshit on a daily basis. Seriously, y'all, she the coolest, most powerful fucking human in existence.

Other Titles from Alexander Nader

Beasts of Burdin Series:

1. Beasts of Burdin
2. Burdin of Choice
3. Burdin's End
4. Demon Days
5. Demon Games (Spring 2022)

Mountain City Chronicles

1. Necrotown
2. Vampire Valley
3. The Glow (Spring 2022)

Stand Alone Titles

Hero Engine

Possessed – A Weird Western

Dirt Road Home – A Young Adult Novel (Coming Soon)

Additional Titles from the Hair Brained Family

The Wrong Side of the Grass: a collection of horror by Parker Jones

Dirk McAwesome and the Giant Fire Breathing Space Ants by Richard Junk

Vampire Valley

Made in the USA
Middletown, DE
21 July 2024